THINKING ABOUT MAGRITTE

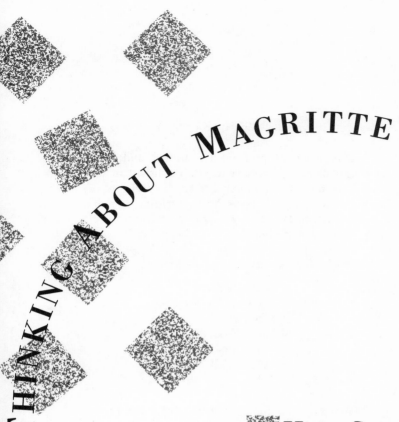

THINKING ABOUT MAGRITTE

Kate Sterns

Pantheon Books   New York

Library of Congress Cataloging-in-Publication Data

Sterns, Kate.
Thinking about Magritte/Kate Sterns.
p.   cm.
ISBN 0-679-41207-7
I. Title.
PR9199.3.S785T48   1992
813'.54—dc20   91-50751

Manufactured in the United States of America
First American Edition

for my parents

I would like to acknowledge my debt to the following people: Sarah, David, Mary, Barbara, Shelagh and Colin, Joanna Labon, Ann and Eugene, Ted, Lucy, Mary Hamilton, Jeannie, Nick, Sue, Rachel Calder, Bill Swainson. Very special thanks to: Heather Wardle, Jo Anne Robertson and Anne Koval.

i

. . . this place is not the sweet home that it looks . . .

from "In Praise of Limestone" by W. H. AUDEN,
Selected Poems

And Ghosts Must Do Again

The Midnight Cowboy never dreamed of machines. What he loved was the blood running past bone of the human body. The fact that a blood cell knew to turn left rather than right. The way veins ran so impossibly close to the surface. The ability of the heart, however broken and scarred, to keep pumping. Against the odds his own had carried him through to his thirtieth year. Hydrocephalus is what the doctors called it. Water on the brain. As a child Cowboy liked to imagine the feel of cool, metal fish slip-slapping against his skull. When he told his mother about this she had placed her ear against the white swell of his forehead.

– I'm listening to the sea, said Lily. I can hear the waves.

Heathen Fictions

T he city, although small, boasted: five prisons, three hospitals, one mental institution and one university. Inhabitants of the place grew up thinking it natural one way or another to enclose and protect people. Nobody escaped attention. All of these buildings were made of the grey, dimpled limestone after which the city was named. Recorded in the history books was a fire which had left the infant city in ruins. It was then they began to construct out of limestone instead of wood. The stone was plentiful and readily quarried. One of the properties of limestone is that it splits easily along its plane of weakness. On occasion absent-minded prison wardens and university professors wandered into the wrong institution, mistaking one for the other. People sailing along the lake glided past the prisons and argued about the cruelty of the correctional system, not realizing that beyond the walls a class in quantum physics was taking place.

The north end of Limestone consisted of a series of haphazard streets, all with the uneven look of a line drawn freehand. They were late additions to the city and unplanned. Towards the end of the nineteenth century an overflow of immigrants and dockworkers, one group attracted to Limestone's prosperity and the other chiefly responsible for creating it, had made them necessary. They used up available space the way spilled water claims a table-top. For most of the immigrants this neighbourhood was no more than a whistle-stop. They moved on quickly to other cities or at least to a better neighbourhood, south of Divide Street, which acted according to its name and split the city down the middle. After a time trains replaced ships as a cheaper and faster means of transport. Limestone began to lose its advantage as a harbour city and the dockers found themselves out of work, consigned to history. Over the next seventy years the north end of the city adopted the grim, concentrated visage of its few remaining tenants. More and more street corners played host to women and children whose husbands and fathers had found temporary accommodation in one of the local prisons. Visitors to Limestone never ventured north of Divide Street except by mistake. Maps of the city grew fuzzy around the edges as if a problem undefined was a problem solved.

Members of Limestone's city council were faced with the daily embarrassment of having to step over drunks and homeless children on their way to work. So a resolution was passed. With the intention of making the streets as clear as their consciences the council magnanimously voted to purchase several of what were, by now, tumbledown houses and donate them to the neighbourhood's indigent population. One of these was No. 22 Colbourne Street, where the Midnight Cowboy had grown up and still lived. The house comprised several stories, most of them untrue. What there was of metal rusted and was never replaced. Plastic sheeting covered several of the windows. The fragile properties of glass were treated with amused contempt by the occupants. On one side was a Chinese laundry and on the other a blind alley. Across the street, visible from Cowboy's second-floor window, was a shoe repair shop, recently gone bust, over which lived Limestone's only prostitute. On slow nights she chatted with Cowboy, but he knew that now was her busy season with one convention after another booked into the Holiday Inn. Reserve prostitutes had been bused in from neighbouring towns for the duration and installed in the less luxurious surroundings of the Plaza Hotel.

– Next week it's chiropractors, Cowboy, she'd yelled earlier, arching her back. Thank God!

Now a light, red and shiny as the inside of an eyelid, winked seductively at a man whose fly was open before he was halfway up the stairs. Before the prostitute had time to produce the American Express/Mastercard/Visa forms the man had flung himself spreadeagled onto the bed. Thinking that for once this might be the real thing formalities were overlooked. The lovers moved in graceful arcs no wider than a belly dancer's hips. They slurped and sucked greedily and the woman wondered why, in the movies, love makes no sound.

The ghosts of Cowboy's childhood lodged amid the cracks in the plaster. They infiltrated the closet. More than once he had removed an article of clothing from the wardrobe only to find a spectre clinging to the sleeve. But tonight there was not a whisper from the living or the dead. The summer heat was democratic in its oppression. Outside the streets were deserted, waiting for the waterfront bars and pool halls to close. In this small corner of the city there was time for affection and violence, that extra glass of beer. Noises (a flash of temper, sneezes, a heavy sigh) lay just outside waiting to be collected by their owners, the last of the heavy drinkers. Rolling and wheezing into the darkness these men and women would reclaim their voices and, fired by drink, catapult them at the windows of their sleeping neighbours. For a few minutes each night all hell broke loose as drowsy arms hurled ancient magazines, sculpted wooden bears, pointed barbs and, once, a live chicken. It was in this way that the neighbourhood's fast-beating heart revealed itself.

★

14

Somewhere in the building a radio was playing. A weather-man, enjoying a fleeting moment of importance, had just concluded that this was the hottest summer the city had experienced since 1922. A heat guaranteed to bruise. Old codgers were interviewed about their recollections of that previous heatwave but chose instead to rant about the immorality of motor cars. The *Limestone Gazette* presented these facts to the public: fifteen dead of sunstroke, 550 gallons of ice cream consumed, 30 percent of the year's barley crop burnt to a cinder. Cowboy himself felt like a piece of white parchment stretched over veins of burning wire. Soon the blackness would spread from the edges to the centre and there would be nothing left of him but ashes.

Four walls are lonely company when they choose to remain silent. There were nights when they told Cowboy stories about his childhood. They told them the way a mother would, making him the central character. His own mother, dead twenty years ago this night, was a practised teller of tales. In this neighbourhood a crumbling anecdote might buy a glass of whiskey or a bed for the night. The stories Lily told to her son were intricately choreographed. They were so familiar that Cowboy could anticipate each turn of phrase, every stitch of embroidery surrounding the truth of the event. Just before her death, when Cowboy was only beginning to understand the limitations of both illness and fairy tales, Lily pointed towards the night sky and the constellations.

– There's fish in heaven, she said. That's where you belong. Most people's lives slant downwards, Cowboy. Think yourself lucky.

Only Lily could have gazed into Cowboy's future and seen a white sheet, neatly tucked at the corners; cool, precise and inviting. Resting his head against the rough wood of the window frame, Cowboy preferred to remember the past.

Evenings when the darkness shrank to the size of the record spinning on the phonograph Lily kept in one corner of the living room. Those were nights reserved for the rhumba and the foxtrot. Sending away a coupon clipped from a woman's magazine, plus $2.75 for postage and handling, Lily received by return post a cardboard box from the Arthur Frobisher Correspondence School of Dance. Inside was a set of orange plastic footprints to be laid on the floor as outlined in the accompanying set of directions. They stretched from the living room through the corridor into the bedroom. (Cowboy once discovered underneath his bed a long-forgotten footprint, like the mark of a one-legged thief.) If the dance was complicated, the Long Island Two-Step or the Matador's Waltz, for example, the footprints detoured into the bathroom. Dip, turn, glide and hold. On paper the principles of the dance seemed easy to grasp. However, the transition from theory to practice was another matter. Somehow Lily always managed to misread a crucial step in the instructions and ended up hopping from one end of the room to the other in a frenzy.

– Never mind, Cowboy, she giggled, we'll make up our own dance.

Then she lifted him up so that his small feet, one of them twisted and near useless, were planted on hers.

– Does this hurt? asked Cowboy.

– I'm crippled, she always answered.

Together they swayed under the moody smile of James Dean, whose picture was taped to the wall.

– He had a voice like Mickey Mouse, sighed Lily. I was crushed.

The needle dug deep into the grooves of the record and chased out the plaintive notes of a Big Bill Broonzy song. It was an old recording, punctuated with rhythmic crack-lings. A favourite joke was to pretend that these static undertones were part of a language only Cowboy could decipher.

– What does the music say? asked Lily.

Why did you trade heaven for these earthly things?

– It says, replied Cowboy, play the game!

Tucking his head under the shelf of her breasts, and with his knees slightly bent for balance, Lily said he looked just like a question mark.

– I got a crazy question between my legs, she laughed.

– What question? demanded Cowboy.

– How many fish in the sea? she asked.

– I know!

– How tall is God?

– I know!

– How many feathers on the wings of an angel?

– I know! I know! I know!

Lily stared into her son's eyes as though they were the walls of an aquarium and soon a rare fish might swim into view.

– You got oysters in your head, she teased, giving you these pearls of wisdom?

– All kinds of fish, answered Cowboy.

From downstairs Mr Murray banged on his ceiling with a broomstick. This was less a signal to stop the music than a plea to be invited up for a mug of gin and a wild thrash in Lily's bed. Thin blades of Blue Grass-scented sweat cut across her face. Lily's body fell easily between the rhythm of the song and the knocking underneath the floor and took her son with her. Just the way she had when she was pregnant with Cowboy and danced with his father that last time.

– What dance are we doing now? she asked. I think we took a detour.

Cowboy pressed his mouth against the soft bulge of Lily's stomach. Their eyes were closed but their feet found the solid places. They avoided the overstuffed armchair and the lamp with Greetings from the Milwaukee Farm Machinery

Fair printed on it. The sound of the banging and all its implications receded. With fingers locked they slid gracefully around the room. The tendrils of their veins intertwined so that, once again, mother and son became one organism.

Lord, Lord, sang Big Bill Broonzy, *It hurts so bad for us to part.*

★　　★　　★

There was a knock at the door and Frank stepped inside. He occupied the room next to Cowboy. During the city's renovations the house was divided and subdivided. Once cheerful apartments, including the one Cowboy had shared with his mother, now wore the forlorn and shabby look of fat men grown suddenly thin. Every floor contained three rooms, each one no bigger than a quilt, and a shared bathroom. The walls were thin and secrets hard to keep.

– Hey, Cowboy, greeted Frank, tapping his forehead, how's the fish?

– I think it's sharks tonight, sighed Cowboy, because something's eating me alive.

Frank nodded in sympathy. He was a big-boned man, generous in form and habit. Curly brown hair, flecked with grey, sprang from almost every available patch of skin so that people got the impression of a benevolent expression without the proof of it. Frank's status as visionary was legend in the building although he never claimed to be a prophet and modestly asserted that anyone could have a vision if they knew where to look. At the age of fifty-four Frank had discovered he was pregnant. On being told the news Cowboy declared:

– The pitter-patter of tiny feet. That's a good thing.

The hallway was crammed with cast-off strollers, gifts from well-wishers. Frank often returned to find one of the

18

tenants, usually Doris, curled up asleep in the three-wheeled baby carriage left outside his door. He simply drew a blanket over the sleeping form, whispered a lullaby and counted it good practice.

– Maxine's got the jiggers tonight, whispered Frank.

– Me too, answered Cowboy.

All night long Cowboy had listened to the sound of Maxine clump, clump, clumping across the floor and knew it was only a matter of time before she came clump, clump, clumping down the stairs to his room. Better than any mind reader Cowboy knew that Maxine was thinking about Old River, her husband, down at the Plaza (unh huh) licking whiskey off the tables. Women loved the dogs of this world and in a room this small there was no escaping a fact like that.

– Savage come looking for you, said Cowboy.

– I been to the hospital, Frank confided.

The Limestone Psychiatric Hospital was an accepted part of Frank's life. He had been an outpatient there for almost as long as Cowboy had been alive on this earth. Small voices had whispered in Frank's ear on and off since he was a boy. At the dinner table his parents might sit there, forks raised halfway to their mouths, as Frank's conversation was hijacked and flown into unknown territories. During these times the whispers would be supplemented by those of men and women in white coats. A polite man, Frank gave equal consideration to the voices inside and outside his head and then pursued his own course. Nobody in the building gave it a second thought. Frank could name the present-day prime minister and that was more than any of them could do.

– What did the doctors say? asked Cowboy.

– They don't believe about the baby, sighed Frank.

Unlike doctors it wasn't in Frank's nature to question miracles or impose definitions.

– The baby's quiet tonight, he said anxiously. Is that good or bad?

– I only know about being born, answered Cowboy.

Upstairs there was a scuffling noise.

– You waiting for Maxine?

– Always, sighed Cowboy.

– Don't carry a torch in this heat, advised Frank.

The front door slammed shut. Cowboy watched from his window as Frank left the house. In the distance a police siren slashed a quick way through the night. Jumping at the noise Frank turned on his heel and headed north, away from the main street. At the first corner was a construction site. Builders had erected a tall fence around it as if their activities were a secret, shameful thing. Of course it was only half a secret. Nobody knew what was being built, just what was torn down. With the curiosity of a child Frank stopped at the fence and put his eye to the peephole. Cowboy, who often lingered there, could have told him that the only thing left was the sign:

LATINI & SONS
SINCE 1861

Two weeks before, in the process of demolishing the shop, workmen discovered the skeleton of a little girl buried in one of the walls. The man who found her had six children of his own and gathered the bones tenderly as if at any moment she might come back to life in his arms. Within minutes the entire neighbourhood was taking bets on how long she'd been there and the cause of death. Old River was convinced she'd been buried alive. Soon everyone had stories to tell of strangled cries in the night and cutlery that walked by itself. Eventually the police, immune to the romance of bones wiped clean of history, came to fetch the skeleton. The *Limestone Gazette* featured the story, beginning with a shrill headline and ending, three days later, with a few lines at the back of the sports section. Although they fall in love every day people grow quickly bored with a mystery they can never solve. Now Cowboy thought of the little girl and understood what it must have been like for the child, ear pressed to the wall and the sounds of the living (a belch, a smacking kiss) reminding her always of what was just beyond reach.

The shop harboured another ghost. It was an incident which occurred when Cowboy was ten years old. Even now the memory was fresh as the scent of ground coffee and lavender that used to fill the premises of Latini & Sons. It had been an old-fashioned general store renowned for the idiosyncrasy of its inventory. Mr Latini, grandson of the original owner, refused to sell anything he did not eat himself. So there were crates of kumquats, baskets of wild mushrooms and an entire section devoted to different varieties of pickled beets. But no beef or Brussels sprouts. In the spring of 1949 the shelves were cleared of all stock that began with the letter "P". Rounds of soft, yellow cheeses were kept behind a glass counter and a sharp knife kept close by for the purpose of cutting off slivers for a trial taste. Framed photographs of the famous people who had patronized the shop hung on the wall. Mr Latini, resplendent in a spotless white apron, pointed with pride to those of Italian extraction who had, along with himself, made good in the new country. Children were drawn to Latini & Sons because of the vast array of sweets. They were displayed in globe jars arranged side by side on the long counter. Glycerine sticks of assorted colours, licorice twists, homemade fudge and lemon sherbets that fizzled on your tongue and made you sneeze. Children always received a generous measure of candy for their allowance. The poorer children, amazed at how far a dime could stretch, were perplexed when their parents could not perform the same

21

feat. But anyone caught shoplifting received a terrible punishment. One summer, when something precious had been taken from him, Cowboy sidled up to the fruit section and attempted to swipe a ripe, juicy peach. Apprehended, he was made to scrub the wooden floors of the shop every evening for a month. Cowboy limped away from the ordeal with a sense of shame ingrained as deeply as the splinters in his palms and knees.

– The problem with you, Cowboy, observed Mr Latini, is that you have no sense of scale. Peaches in exchange for a dead mother is not a good deal. Have a kumquat.

★　　★　　★

– I come down to you, whispered Maxine.

Despite the heat Cowboy buttoned his shirt right up to the neck. The water in his head rose with the temperature. It bubbled over and rolled down the pale slope of his forehead. Maxine always said that men were equal parts water and shit and tonight this seemed an unbeatable fact. He tried to keep his mind in a space that was preacher clean. Maxine could read his thoughts too easy.

– Come in, he called.

It was nearly fifteen years since Maxine and Old River had moved into the house. Two suitcases and a plastic shopping bag bound with twine were what they'd brought with them. Over the years they'd managed to lose all that and more and they didn't even have the sense to wave goodbye. On that first day Cowboy peered out at the newcomers and saw a young girl of maybe seventeen years, newly married. Black hair lazy as a cat across her shoulders. Maxine always swore no Native blood but Cowboy knew damn sure there was. His heart had traced the sharp and delicate planes of wide shoulders tapering to the waist. White skin split by a knotted rope of backbone.

22

– Ride it easy, Cowboy.

Maxine had a shapeless voice. It could be belted tight or left loose and easy depending on the occasion. At this moment it was whiskey tight and that meant trouble.

– OK, Maxine?

– Cowboy, she said, I saw a woman today all covered in leaves. Different kinds. Oak, maple, birch. She was sittin' on a bench still as a dead heart. I stood in front of her lookin' and lookin'. With my whole body I was askin' her why? She says, I'm a tree *stoopid*.

Story over, Maxine brought her arms forward, palms toward the floor, and then dropped them back by her side. The tips of her fingers were rust coloured.

– You dancing with crazy tonight? enquired Cowboy.

Leaning over, Maxine hissed:

– You are so fuckin' clumsy, Cowboy! I make a space for you here (indicating her heart) and you keep bumping into things and making me mad.

– Sorry, sniffed Cowboy.

– You ever seen an animal without its skin? she demanded.

– You mean a skeleton?

– Yeah.

– I seen skeletons, he answered. So?

– Everything looks mean skinned to the bone, explained Maxine. I'm just barely skin and bone tonight, Cowboy. Don't make me out mean.

– Everything that dies comes back one way or another, comforted Cowboy.

– You think so? she asked.

– See that crane hunched against the moon? he said, pointing over the road. It looks just like a dinosaur. An old thing in a new body. Everything comes back.

– I hope so, she sighed.

The bed springs creaked as Maxine sat down. Cowboy

couldn't decide whether she weighed more or was just weighed down. Marriage always seemed a heavy load for Maxine to carry.

– Hey, Cowboy, she grinned, bouncing up and down, I'm giving away memories tonight. Here's one for you.

– What?

– I was thinking of that night you serenaded me. Maybe nine years ago. You wore my best dress.

A yellow cotton with black buttons. He'd stolen it from the clothesline. It was still damp as he pulled it on over his head. Even after all this time it was a source of satisfaction to Cowboy to recall how well the dress had clung to his gaunt frame.

– I looked good, smiled Cowboy.

– You really needed tits and hips to do it right, commented Maxine. I'll never forget it. Lookin' out into the backyard and seein' you standing there on that old toilet we threw away. The moon was out full and you were singing . . . What was that song?

– Thought you said you'd never forget, remarked Cowboy.

– Just the name of the song.

– "Since I Fell For You", he sighed.

– Oh yeah. And everyone was leaning out of the window and gawping. Frank got stuck and it took a whole tub of margarine to get him loose.

– And Old River started yelling how he was going to come downstairs and kick my ass, added Cowboy.

– He was laughing too hard to do any serious damage.

– *I* didn't know that.

– I warned you, Cowboy. Love's a bony thing sometimes, you're liable to get an eye poked or a rib cracked.

– Yeah, well, thanks for the memory, Maxine.

– Hey, Cowboy?

– What?

– I think I've really lost him this time.

– Old River's down at the Plaza, Cowboy assured her, like every night.

– I want him back.

– You want me to look for him, Maxine, or what?

– Be my baby, Cowboy, she pleaded. Find him for me.

Dead flies lined the window ledge. The curl of their bodies made it look like they'd been praying when they fell. Absentmindedly flicking them over the edge Cowboy also offered a short prayer. "Now I lay me down to sleep" was the only one he knew, but it seemed appropriate. The insects made a gratifying click as they ricocheted off the curve of his fingernail in the direction of Leon's Kosher Chinese Take-Away. It was the usual culprit when it came to the vermin and strange odours infesting the street. The window was darkened but Cowboy caught a glimpse of Leon sitting at a makeshift table with his family. They ate their dinner each night after closing. It was a safe bet that Leon was forced to open a restaurant just to feed all his relatives. Apart from the rest of the family, shelling peas, sat the aged grandmother. She had very, very small feet. Frank, who knew about these things, explained that in China young women used to have their feet broken and then bound tight to make them tiny. Every time the grand-mother hobbled out onto the street Cowboy watched her progress anxiously, convinced that eventually she would topple over. A grandmother with a good-sized pair of feet was one less worry on a man's mind.

– Surrounded by falling women, thought Cowboy.

It was the thin, curved back of love that got him every time.

Emily Brontë Sings Country
and Western

Around the corner from No. 22 Colbourne Street Ernie was engaged in conversation with a cat.

– I wonder how *my* mother would look stuffed, he mused.

When he saw Cowboy limping towards him, Ernie made a space for him on the curb. To Ernie's way of thinking there was something of the cartoon ghost about Cowboy. Maybe it was the bulbous head, the deathly pale skin and the way his body shrank to nothing. Also, the twisted leg meant that Cowboy bobbed along the surface of the earth rather than having his feet planted firmly on it. As Cowboy took the place offered on the curb he noticed the violin resting on Ernie's lap.

– Play something, he requested.

Ernie frowned, shook his head and pointed towards the cat.

– It's strung with a relative, he admonished.

They observed a few moments of silence. If you said something it had to mean something and they wanted to remain undefined for awhile. In spite of his youth (the cat had more whiskers) Ernie was regarded as the religious man of the community. His father was a fundamentalist lay-preacher in a small town whose population swelled each weekend with the arrival of miners from a nearby camp. These men knew the earth's heat first-hand and laughed at the Preacher's depictions of fire and brimstone. At first his congregation was so small that meetings were held in the back of his Chevrolet automobile. In the mornings Ernie would bring his father a cup of tea to find the Preacher wiggling his toes, a slight transgression in his youth having left him with a phobia of waking up paralysed. He was considering the problem of how to fill his quota for the Lord.

A solution was reached the year Ernie turned twelve. Outraged by the naked greed he saw displayed on any of the twenty game shows broadcast daily on commercial television, the Preacher began bombarding the winning contestants with letters. He directed them to surrender their ill-gotten gains to the church.

– A washing machine obtained through avarice, he wrote, will never make you clean.

The media picked up on the Preacher's campaign and soon there was a steady stream of washer-dryers, toasters and golf-clubs coming into the house. One couple had won a trip to Hawaii and didn't see how they could give that back but would their sofa, almost new, suffice? It was Ernie's job to redirect the appliances to orphanages and hospitals, although he held on to one vacuum cleaner and an electric carving knife and hoped that the Lord wouldn't mind. Gradually the producers of the most popular gameshows began to get worried. There were still plenty of people applying to appear on the programmes but instead of jumping up and down the contestants were apologetic. Some wore wigs and gave false names. Winners cowered shamefaced by their letter-boxes waiting for the Preacher's denunciations of their wicked ways. Even atheists found it difficult to look their neighbours squarely in the eye. Eventually the producers travelled cap in hand to the Preacher. They promised him his own church and a spanking new Chevrolet if he agreed to abandon his missive warfare. The Preacher shook each of their hands in turn and said they had a deal.

The only thing Ernie took away from the church, besides a crate of communion wine, was a love of music. The Preacher had bought him a cheap violin so that he could accompany the sermon with antiseptic renditions of popular psalms. For the most part Ernie complied but there were moments when his mind wandered away from God and his fingers followed. Then "Nearer My God To Thee" got hot and sticky. When the Preacher got his own church Ernie switched to the organ but no matter how much passion Ernie brought to his playing the sound always chilled him to the bone. It made his heart heavy and belied the notion that it was uplifting music. He saw reflected in the burnished pipes a picture of the congregation sinking through the floorboards, the music a giant finger poking them down, down, down. The notes became jumbled, traitors to good intentions. In an effort to raise the congregation and forestall the Preacher's inevitable wrath Ernie played circus music and television theme tunes. The music whirled around the church like a figure skater but cut no ice with the Preacher.

– You disgraced me, hissed the Preacher.

– The congregation was sinking fast, answered Ernie. I was trying to save them.

– That's *my* job, responded the Preacher.

Over the seven years Ernie had lived in Limestone he'd devoted himself to building a church organ in his bedsitting room. The parts were carefully culled from various sources. Some of the wood came from a church abandoned by everyone except an old man who brought a fresh bunch of wild flowers every day. The metal was stripped from the Studebaker in which Ernie's neighbour had conceived her daughter. When it was finished, although smaller than a regular church organ, it took up nearly half of Ernie's room. Once a month, never on Sunday, he invited friends from all the dust-ridden nooks and crannies of his life to a recital. Wearing a dinner jacket stolen from a church bazaar, he played hymns learned at his father's knee. It gave Ernie a devious thrill to steal this music back from God for the pleasure of his pals, who, more often than not, fell asleep. While they snored peacefully in the corner Ernie remained seated at the organ. The only thing that matched his love for music was the heroic amount of tequila he consumed. Ernie liked the transmutability of this liquor, the way it changed from smooth glass to cut glass inside his stomach. At a certain point in the evening Ernie could always count on hearing his father's voice.

– You drink too much, roared the Preacher.

– I know, agreed Ernie. Please don't shout.

– These concerts are blasphemous, continued the Preacher. What will God say?

– He says nothing, sighed Ernie, grasping a fistful of his blond curls and pulling hard in irritation. Not a word.

In the gospel according to Ernie religion was a brick wall. All your life you knocked against it and when it finally collapsed it fell the wrong way and buried you alive.

The cat decided to leave.

– Three's a crowd, it said.

– Bye, cat! shouted Ernie, waving until the animal was out of sight.

The cat looked lonely and Ernie had devoted several hours of his company to it. Still, he was not hurt at being abandoned. Ernie was in no way territorial. He turned to Cowboy and gave him the full one-two of his blue eyes.

– Nice outfit, Cowboy, he remarked.

It was a tribute to Carmen Miranda minus the hat. A tight red bolero matched with trousers, which jumped from the ledge of his hips and landed in a frothy black pool at his feet.

– You seen Old River tonight, Ernie?

– Maxine send you out looking?

– Yeah.

– Cowboy, declared Ernie, one day doctors are going to cut you open and they'll find Maxine's teeth marks all over your heart.

– She's sharp tonight, agreed Cowboy.

A goldfish floated behind Cowboy's left eye and imparted an incandescent light to the grim and lopsided houses that lined the street. It reminded him of the yellowing photographs his mother had kept. When Lily first became ill she spent more and more evenings wrapped in an old bathrobe, propped against a pile of cushions on the sofa. Open on her lap was a leatherbound album. The thing Cowboy noticed most about these photographs was that the camera did not look for indiscretions: the blurred hand caught replacing a loose wisp of hair, or eyes half closed. The subjects of these photos were prepared. They faced the camera and smiled, confident in their ability to transcend the years intact. Sometimes, Lily bent so low over these snapshots that Cowboy was afraid of losing her entirely to the past and grabbed her hand in panic. Smiling, she fingered the curled edges of the photographs and said:

– Innocence belongs to this colour.

Then she pointed to her favourite photograph.

– This is me, she whispered. This is what I look like.

Her hair was freshly cut in a pageboy, the bangs a straight line across her forehead, like the mark a mother makes on the wall to determine how much a child has grown each year. Invisible to the camera were the snippets of hair which stuck to the back of her neck or slipped to the moist place between her shoulderblades and tickled her. Both corners of the dress (Gingham, said Lily. But it probably wasn't. She just liked the word.) were held primly between forefinger and thumb. The dress was spread out so that Lily looked like a triangle with legs. She faced the camera with the wariness of a six-year-old whose older brothers were always pointing things at her: sticks, toy guns, swords, her role being then to fall down obediently and play dead. Now her father was directing her to stand up straight and smile. Eager to please (unlike the dress and her shyness in front of the camera this was never outgrown), Lily lifts her chin and grins.

– When I first saw this picture, she told Cowboy, I thought it was a miracle. I thought how wonderful that a box could hold your life like that. I'd never seen anyone buried. I didn't know about dying.

There was a slight sensation as the goldfish nibbled on the lens of Cowboy's eye, which filled with tears.

– Can you hear the fish? whispered Cowboy.

Ernie came close as two-part harmony and listened.

– All quiet, he announced. The tide must be out.

Somewhere Ernie had read that you could tell if a man or woman was close to death by examing the whites of their eyes. They became completely clear so that their last view of the world was unobstructed. Whenever he travelled on public transport Ernie checked the state of his neighbour's eyes. Only when he'd reassured himself that they were mean, veined and tired as his own, concentrating on crying babies and cheap novels, did he allow himself to sit comfortably. Looking into Cowboy's eyes was to see two white sails with a black hole burned into the centre of each.

– I'm dying every day, confided Cowboy, who knew of Ernie's fixation.

– You're OK, Cowboy.

– Ernie, he asked, will I be a cripple in heaven?

– Oh fuck, Cowboy, groaned Ernie. Ask my father.

– I don't want a book idea of heaven, pleaded Cowboy, placing his hand against Ernie's heart.

31

– I think you'll be an angel, pronounced Ernie, and all angels are crippled because they love God too much.

– You'll be an angel too, said Cowboy, anxious to share his good fortune.

– I'm no angel, laughed Ernie, I just act like one.

(The moon sat like a fat-legged child on the dome of the city hall.)

– Listen, said Ernie, I'll tell you my dream. I walk into a room full of people I recognize. Using sign language I begin to expound the theory of relativity. I employ only the most simple of gestures, but when I come to the heart of it I'm afraid we'll all be drowned by the weight of this genius cascading from my fingertips. Then I look up and realize that all they see is a man waving his arms around. Well, I think to myself, this is the last party *you* get invited to.

Silence often counterfeits understanding, so Cowboy merely smiled encouragingly and twiddled his thumbs. Meanwhile Ernie shuddered as though pierced by the sting of a thousand bees searching frantically for honey. He picked up the violin and rose to his feet.

– Where are you going? asked Cowboy.

– If I hurry I can catch the one o'clock train, said Ernie.

In the early days of Limestone transport was confined mainly to steamships. The *Limestone Gazette* maintained that this form of transport was outdated. It was better suited to a moral climate in which shipboard tomfoolery was tolerated. In a modern age businessmen want speed, not kisses. Limestone needed a railway. Surveys were taken and revealed rich deposits of minerals along the planned route. Ores with names like opera singers: galena, plumbago, mica. A member of parliament travelled up from the capital to drive in the first spike. Ale, beef and homemade blueberry pies were served. Speeches were made about the great wealth Limestone would enjoy once it was connected with the reserves of natural resources to the north. A brass band played. For posterity a photograph was taken of the railway crew. They were a motley assortment of young men in their twenties. String was tied around the waist of their trousers to hold them up. One of them still had a slice of pie in his hand when the flash went off. All of them wore smiles of unrepentant blue.

In April of 1890 the first train left Limestone station. The mayor's wife presented the driver with a gift of red velvet curtains to mark the event. Unable to refuse, the driver hung them to a round of polite applause. The curtains became a talking point of every railway depot within a five-hundred-mile radius. All this embittered the driver to the extent that he refused to stop at Limestone. He merely slowed the train. The first few passengers watched in disbelief as the platform came into view and then receded into the distance. However, the next station was over an hour away so one day a passenger with a pressing engagement that afternoon simply jumped. He threw out his luggage, said a quick prayer and leapt into the goldenrod growing by the tracks. This audacious feat was greeted with admiration and the next day no fewer than ten passengers disembarked the same way. This continued to be the policy until the driver retired. In lieu of a gold watch the railway company presented him with the red curtains. Two months later he was killed by a bull. The curtains were found torn and bloodstained at his side.

On the centenary of the station's opening a new set of curtains was hung and the policy of slowing down, but not stopping, reinstated. Old women climbed onto the backs of male students and tumbled down the embankment. They were reminded of a time long ago when they had lain breathless under the weight of a young man. Every so often Ernie would hike to the station, carrying his violin, and wait for the arrival of the train. He observed as passengers threw themselves like brightly coloured confetti from the passing locomotive. It was a contest to see which ones, under difficult circumstances, were able to land with dignity.

Ernie scooped up Cowboy's hand in his own and lightly kissed it. As he retreated down the street he was pursued by compliments.
– You have a lovely nose! Your tomato pie is wonderful!
But they soon got tired of chasing him and spent the night in a deserted alley.

La Petite Rêve

The way to the Plaza Hotel was long and hazardous. It could be approached directly from Divide Street but Cowboy preferred a more roundabout route. Because he moved slowly Cowboy was a popular target for local boys who had nothing better to do on a Saturday night than chase cripples. They drove along in their cars, streetlights easing along chrome, and chased him down. Whenever Cowboy went out unaccompanied at night he instinctively rounded his slight shoulders, pinning his arms to hips which lost their exaggerated swing. Veering east after leaving Colbourne Street, Cowboy headed towards the waterfront by a series of darkened side streets, unlocked garden gates and fire escapes until he found himself in front of a small, clapboard building on a rundown corner of MacDonald and Arthur. Cowboy did not intend to visit this place tonight. Maybe it was the heat poking a finger in his back and pushing him forward against his will. One thing was clear: sent out to look for one thing you invariably found another. Reach under the bed for a shoe and you pulled out a half-eaten sandwich.

RAINBOW HOUSE OF BEAUTY
(Where Looking Good Doesn't Cost a Pot of Gold)

The sign could barely be read now but Cowboy knew it from the days when it had a fresh coat of paint every spring.

His neighbour, Doris, who owned the business, had sold it to a land developer five years ago when all her hair fell out.

– A bald beautician doesn't inspire confidence, Cowboy, she sighed.

The premises were now as derelict as its former customers.

The phantom of Mrs Munscher, electrocuted by a rogue hairdryer in 1969, swung moodily on the gate. She quickly divined Cowboy's intentions.

– Don't go in there, she warned.

– I'm looking for Lily, he explained.

– You promised your mother you'd never set foot in the Rainbow House of Beauty, countered Mrs Munscher, as she inspected her nails.

– Besides, she went on, poking him in the chest, you're doing a lot of looking tonight.

– One thing for me, said Cowboy, and one for Maxine.

– Stick to the living, advised Mrs Munscher, they leave more clues. Lily's buried treasure.

– Just one minute inside, begged Cowboy, that's all I want.

– I'm only a ghost, she pointed out. I can't stop you.

A hole in the screen door made entering a simple matter of sticking his hand through and flipping the catch. With a sense of discretion entirely lacking through the term of her natural life, Mrs Munscher turned her back. She did not have to witness his betrayal, the floorboards creaked heavily beneath the weight of it. As with most forbidden childhood places the room was smaller than Cowboy had imagined. Against the wall were fixed three large white sinks littered with empty plastic squeeze bottles. Their acidic contents had bitten into the porcelain like bad-tempered animals. Stacks of mildewed magazines were left piled in one corner. The mirrors were cracked, the work of teenagers who felt beyond the reach of superstition but who wore their lucky jacket on an important date. Cowboy ran his fingers over dusty surfaces. He imagined the network of women who had found sanctuary here from the restless world outside. Dirty jokes and family secrets being freely exchanged as the women slung their legs across the arms of their chairs. Cigarette smoke curled in thick profusion above their heads as Doris dealt expertly with split-ends and wilted permanents. Her rough but affecting voice sang songs of no-good, faithless men to loud applause. They called her the human radio because she could imitate any popular singer, from Rosemary Clooney to Fats Waller.

– I'll entertain requests, she'd joke, but just dinner and a movie.

Lily looked for the smell of her own skin until the day she died. Almonds, peaches and jojoba were the price she paid for a steady job at the Rainbow House of Beauty. Every morning clients waited there like ducks, their necks resting on arches of white porcelain, for Lily's fingers to turn them into swans. In the evening after work she slipped into the back room and sniffed at her arms and hands. Always on her skin was the faint smell of the promises she'd sold that day. Yes! This lotion will make you look younger. Yes! This hairstyle will make your husband love you. Always on her skin the promise of a better life for someone else.

She was eighteen years old, all red mouth and springtime hips, when she met Cowboy's father. He was a long-haul truck driver and brought to bed with him the sights and sounds of wherever he'd been. Under her pillow Lily might find a grain of wheat, a jar of mountain air or sometimes an entire salmon. Like jazz they sank into long, hot nights of playing fast and loose. One night she discovered a small patch of white, the size of a nickel, nestled in the deep tan of the truck driver's thigh. With a ballpoint pen she branded

her initials onto the circle of his skin. LJM. Lily Jane Mac-
Dougall.

– You belong to me, she breathed.

Sweetly she lay her nose against his back, stomach, shoulder and made a search for her own smell.

– I don't know where I lost it, she'd say. I just don't
know where it went.

But the truck driver wasn't giving anything away. His
attention began to splinter and cut Lily as she moved against
him. Pretty soon he got sick of her sniffing like a dog. Got
sick of smelling nothing but almonds, peaches, jojoba, and
stepped out the door. All he left her was the salmon and a
belly shouldering its way into air.

– I don't mind, she said. All I want is something that
smells like itself. That's all I want now.

When Cowboy was born Lily buried her face in the exotic
human fragrance of the child. Her nose became a guide to
loving her son. Scented soaps, perfumes and powders were
banned. The Rainbow House of Beauty was off limits.
Cowboy grew used to waking in the middle of the night
only to find Lily with her nose pressed against his skin
breathing deeply. His odour acted on her like a drug. Social
workers paid visits in an effort to convince Lily that she was
required by law to send Cowboy to school. They believed
she was worried about the other children's reactions to
Cowboy's freakish appearance. This thought had never
occurred to Lily.

– He'd end up smelling like other kids, she explained,
and I'd never find him again.

– The place has gone to seed, admitted Mrs Munscher.

– I never saw it before, reminded Cowboy.

– You find what you wanted? she enquired politely.

– No, he sighed. Lily's not here.

38

– I stick to places I know, volunteered Mrs Munscher, but your mother was more adventurous.

– Oh, said Cowboy.

Glancing into a remaining fragment of mirror, Mrs Munscher plucked a stray hair from her chin.

– Listen, she began, I came into the Rainbow House of Beauty wanting to look like Grace Kelly.

– Unh huh? murmured Cowboy.

– We don't always get what we want, snapped Mrs Munscher. Say hi to Doris for me.

Sing What Your Voice
Come to Most

The architect of the Limestone Psychiatric Hospital was often accused of making symbolic gestures. Mr Atkinson was only thirty-five when, in 1920, the first stone was laid but he maintained the attire of a Victorian gentleman.

– This is a disgraceful era, he complained. I'm here against my will.

Faced with a battery of raised eyebrows at the city council meeting, the mayor pointed out that genius always demands generous leeway.

The proposed location for the new asylum was a prime piece of waterfront property, slightly diminished in value due to its proximity to the men's penitentiary. The *Limestone Gazette* insinuated that the property had been donated to the city by the wealthy family of a prominent politician, now broken under the strain of public life, in exchange for a room in the asylum. Every morning dozens of convicts who were to engage in the actual construction were transported to the site under the watchful eyes of their keepers. Regulations stipulated that work was to be carried out in absolute silence although the phrase "Look out!" was occasionally permitted, more for the safety of the keepers than the prisoners. Mr Atkinson found the atmosphere so oppressive that he developed the habit of wandering among the men under the guise of inspecting sewage pipes and cornices, distributing notes hastily scribbled from one prisoner to another. By this means love affairs flourished, political debates raged and rumours were circulated. One of these involved the news that the asylum, on account of the politician, was to hire a French chef. Bearing this in mind, several of the prisoners did everything in their power to recommend themselves as potential patients. One man persistently mistook a dead chicken for a hammer, while another staged impromptu performances of *Swan Lake*.

– These lunatics will ruin the asylum, giggled Mr Atkinson.

When the building was completed the critics (no one asked the certifiably insane) were delighted. They spent weeks unearthing clues they imagined Mr Atkinson had left for them in his design. For example, although the hospital was constructed almost entirely of limestone there were one or two fissures where wood and brick had been allowed to take hold.

– Might this not represent, they slyly commented, the cracked minds of the patients?

On hearing this, the architect kissed his parrot (named Chat Lunatique) and lamented.

– Why, he wondered, do all critics smell of ashes and gin?

In addition, the path leading from the main building, set in the centre of a great estate, was long and winding.

Surely, the critics claimed, this is a metaphor for the arduous journey between madness and sanity.

Throughout his long life the architect vigorously denied these charges.

*   *   *

The moon looked down on two figures lying on a dark prickle of grass known to the residents of the north end of Limestone as the Park. Once there had been a tree, but it grew so battle-scarred from lovers carving their initials in the trunk, and then crossing them out again after a quarrel, that it keeled over one night during a thunderstorm. These days there was nothing more than a rusted bench, a few shrubs and a convenient resting place for those who lost their way home in the dark. The City Hall clock was striking one, closely followed by the bells of St Michael's church. For as long as anyone could remember these institutions had run a fierce race for the role of official timekeeper. Frank pictured the mayor waddling furiously towards the finish line with a red-robed bishop close behind.

– It's seven months now, he said, and I still haven't thought what to call the baby.

– What about Savage? suggested his companion.

– But it's your name, protested Frank, I want one that's brand new.

Frank's father, a builder of roads during the depression, had always stressed the value of a child's name.

– If it's strong, he maintained, it will help you rise above hard times.

His own name was Oswald, but he called himself the exception that proves the rule.

– Jiggerbugger's a new name, Frank.

Savage howled as Frank turned and bit him on the shoulder.

– Jesus! cried Savage. Anyway I don't see why you need a kid when you already got me.

– I love you, Frank comforted, but you're not flesh. Flesh is what I need to hold me together.

Like a bear in the circus Frank spent his days riding around and around on a bicycle. As he rode he looked neither to the right nor the left but into any one of the hundred mirrors he had fixed to the bike.

– I like to piece the world together as I go, he explained.

This was how he and Savage had met.

– You'll have to fuckin' piece *me* together, Savage had yelled as Frank rode over him.

Frank peered over his handlebars at the skinny kid with fresh tire marks across his stomach. He had a look that could cut you down cool and fast as a knife. One ear was pulled lower than the other. This was the result of a father who, Frank found out later, saw the world distorted through the convex glass of a bottle and shaped his son's ear to fit.

– Who are you? asked Frank.

– Savage, came the reply.

The word barely licked Frank's ear it was spoken so softly.

– Sandwich?

– SAVAGE!

This became something regular with Savage. His first words were a trial jump, barely getting off the ground. You'd think he was dying of consumption, his strength sapped and then, whoosh!, he left you for dust.

– What are you doing lying in the middle of the park? enquired Frank.

– Catching pigeons, answered Savage.

– Why?

– I sell the meat.

Although only twelve years old, Savage knew how to keep silent and wait. He understood the essential trick to catching birds was to take pleasure in the seduction not the killing. He had a talent for it and rarely left the park empty-handed.

– Oh, said Frank.

– What are you doing here, Savage asked, besides trying to kill me?

– I'm taking the baby for a ride.

– What baby? demanded Savage.

– This one, said Frank proudly, pointing to his belly. Savage gave him the sharp eye.

– You from the Loony Tin? he asked.

– Sometimes, said Frank. I come and go. Talking of Michelangelo.

– What?

– It's a poem.

– How do you know poetry?

– I had to have a life to make a life, reasoned Frank.

– How come you're having a baby? persisted Savage.

– I don't know, admitted Frank. I had a vision. It just come to me.

– Like pigeons, agreed Savage, they just come to me too.

– It's a good thing, smiled Frank.

Truth may be constant, but people choose what they want to believe in this world. Craziness could tilt a man to one side and knock him off his feet. Savage had seen that often enough in this neighbourhood. But here was the balance of the world. One man waiting for a thing to be born while at his side another man helps a thing to die. Savage trusted that there were times to place the fictions of life above the facts.

– I'll feed it, said Frank. I'll take it to the park.

– You'll have to learn a whole new language, cautioned Savage.

– This baby, Frank had assured him, will be pure, sweet genius.

Savage understood that there were times when Frank looked down and saw nothing but hard ground and only the baby to break his fall. He picked up a stray leaf which had fluttered onto his bare arm. He rolled it between his thumb and forefinger until it was a spindle of green slime. Even in the dark, Savage knew what things looked like dead. He liked to know what to expect.

– You seen Cowboy tonight? asked Savage.

– Yeah, answered Frank. Maxine's got him on the hook.

– You ever watched a pigeon close? asked Savage. They

44

kind of make a run at you and then veer off to the side. After a bit they get to running around in little circles, their eyes staring out of their head. Pigeons is always looking for something, food or a place to roost.

– When it comes to pigeons, declared Frank, you are a scholar.

– What I'm saying, continued Savage, Maxine is like those pigeons. Flappin' around. Lookin' for this. Lookin' for that.

– I do my share, said Frank. Cowboy too.

– Maybe, replied Savage, but Maxine's the only one that craps over everyone while she's doing it.

– I feel sorry for her, confessed Frank.

Closing his eyes Frank stretched out his arm and placed his hand against Savage's forehead. With their ankles just touching Frank could see in his mind's eye the cool geometry of the triangle they made.

– Hey, Frank, said Savage, I'm hungry.

– If you got money we could go to Libra's, suggested Frank.

Checking his pockets Savage withdrew a bill and some change. Angling his palm into the moonlight he counted a five-dollar bill and some quarters.

– Luck buys you French fries and coffee, Frank.

– And milk for the baby?

– Anything you want, promised Savage, and extended a hand to help Frank rise.

The Blue Noon

T wo angels were sitting on a rope. They were suspended high in the air (as angels should be) so that below them lay the wrinkled contours of the earth. If they swung left their feet hung over the muddy Mississippi. If they swung to the right they hovered above Hudson Bay.

– I like the sweep of it, remarked the younger angel (still new to the position), it's the details I miss. I think about the hunchback look of bread fresh from the oven. The bone-white of my baby's first tooth.

The more experienced angel, whose name was Oswald, shook his head and sighed. He knew that a successful suspension depended on preserving a precarious balance between aerodynamics and faith. An egg poised on the limpid silver of a teaspoon. He did not want a bout of homesickness to send them hurtling into the Rocky Mountains.

– Man is a giddy thing, quoth Oswald.

On earth his job had been to pave the way from city to city. Now he dealt with journeys of a different kind. Oswald delicately removed a shoe so that a few stray pieces of gravel were released into space.

His accident had occurred over forty years ago but the particulars of it remained strong in his mind. The entire neighbourhood had been witness. The sound of the car hitting the body shattered eyes left and right so that everyone had

46

a different picture of it. Oswald remembered being thrown high as a voice can go before losing its way and then dropped back down. Where the nose had been was a bubble of blood.

– A clown, Frank said. That's not my father. No, no.

Men learn to fill the spaces in their lives the best way they can. People laughed at his son but what did that matter? If balance was a matter of faith then Frank's mind was better balanced than most.

– Come on, Lily, said Oswald, I want to see Africa.

The angels gripped the rope and swung out hard.

In the Cradle Where it Lies

I n the early part of the nineteenth century the *Limestone Gazette* launched a campaign, led by the wife of the proprietor, to clean up the city. A conscientious journalist had uncovered the fact that Limestone sheltered no fewer than seventy-two taverns and five houses of ill repute. The pious citizens of Limestone at first looked to the upright clergy to address the twin evils of drink and prostitution. After an evening spent touring the taverns and brothels, however, the clergy were no longer upright and so nothing came of this. Next, wearing the permanently distracted look of those who keep one eye on heaven and the other on their reputation, the worthy matrons of the Women's Benevolent Association rushed into the fray.

– You're on a downward course, they thundered to a captive audience of drinkers, and you'd better do something about it!

In the knowledge that a convincing portrait of repentance was good for a small piece of silver, some men and women kept disguises stashed at various taverns and timed their visits to coincide with those of the Women's Benevolent Association. On a good night an enthusiastic penitent might earn the price of a bottle of gin.

One of the establishments untouched by either a sense of contrition or the developer's wrecking ball was the Plaza Hotel. It was a dog's mouth: dark, wet and open most of the time. Upstairs rooms were rented by the hour and guests brought no luggage, only protective devices. During the night women with legs like badly rolled cigarettes patrolled the corridors while men with funny hats ducked furtively in and out of the rooms. Occasionally a fight broke out and the manager was summoned. He was a former professional stuntman and had witnessed many things in his lifetime (the death of Hollywood, the spontaneous combustion of a train spotter from Arizona) and knew what to do. Like commitment he came between the man and woman until differences were resolved and the hotel was once more awash with the sound of things going bump in thee night.

In the basement of the hotel was the Plaza bar. Its position on the waterfront meant that originally it was a haven for Irish immigrants, sailors and travelling salesmen. Not only were the present clientele less transient, it was often difficult to remove them from the premises at all. The front room was about twenty yards deep and another fifteen wide. Tables were angled at distances which allowed a man to fall insensible from his chair without disturbing the other drinkers. A beaded curtain separated the front room from the back, where there was a pool table. Sawdust covered the floor to soak up whatever could not be contained. On average, once a night someone would be drunk enough to unzip his trousers and piss against the side of the wall. When this happened the barman retrieved a bucket of antiseptic kept ready for the purpose and heaved it at the offending spot. Entering the Plaza bar a stranger was hit with two smells, one human and one a disguise.

Maxine ordered a beer. As her thighs spread over the edge of the bar stool she recognized that it wasn't just her figure she was losing. Among other things words had lately begun to slip away from familiar meanings and there seemed little point in calling them back. There were words that went fast of their own accord (table, love, marriage) while others (knife, snake, beer) hung around a bit longer.

It was Old River who taught her to drink beer. That was when they were in high school, back when he was still known to the world as Adam Whitelake. Underage and unafraid, he'd walked into the general store and returned a few minutes later with a six-pack. Leading Maxine by the hand he took the path down to the river. In the tall grass Adam opened two of the bottles with his teeth, one of them chipped from the habit, and offered a beer to Maxine. She admired the delicate gold liquid encased in green glass. It reminded her of the corn fields in summer lining the highway and stretching farther than her imagination would ever take her. As Maxine drank she sensed Adam's eyes on her. They followed the trail the beer took from where her lips encircled the mouth of the bottle right down to where it swilled around in her stomach.

– If I were on fire, she thought, he'd sit there just for the pleasure of watching me burn.

Adam broke off a cat-tail and rubbed the brown velvet pad against his cheekbone like it was a real animal and not a namesake.

– I'm angry all the godammed time, he confessed.

– I know, said Maxine.

The first thing she ever noticed about Adam Whitelake was that the blood ran thick in him. He was undiluted. In their small farming town (one bank, one store, six churches) almost everyone was related. Blood was as thin and spread out as their speech. Adam was the new boy in school. He kept himself close as a fist and it wasn't until that day in biology class that Maxine got a good look. One of the students had brought in his pet boa constrictor. The class listened attentively while he spoke of breeding patterns and bible stories. When the student was finished he cleared his throat and asked if anyone wanted to hold it? There was an uneasy silence as the rest of the class shrank back in their seats. A snake had brought sin into the life of man and that was a terrible burden to carry on your shoulders. In the end it was Adam that stepped forward. A man who in later life would cower behind a whiskey bottle now stood there confidently cradling his own downfall. Maxine decided there and then that bravery was just well-intentioned stupidity. The skin of the snake was dry as the nose of a sick dog, cracked and leathery. Every time it moved there was a dangerous twitch of muscle. Both Adam and the snake possessed a quality that Maxine could not identify but would come to know by heart. If they killed you it would not be out of hate, which you could recognize and run from, only carelessness. Everything about Adam was careless, from the swept-back greasy black hair to the broken shoe-laces held together with knots. Girls were always whispering about him in the change room. Secretly they thought of what sex with Adam (which they never pictured as a prolonged act but as a series of interruptions) would be like. At birth they were presented with a clear picture of their life: school, marriage and children. The background changed but the smiling girl in the middle never did. It was exciting to dream about a boy whose coarse bristles against their breast, whose hand up their skirt, direct but not brutal, would throw things out of focus for awhile. They endowed his apparent laziness with a rebel spirit. Only Maxine suspected that Adam had been dealt a surplus of energy and a brain that offered limited options on how to use it.

What Maxine never saw was the way Adam opened his mouth wide to the snake. If she'd been paying attention she could have grabbed hold and pulled it out. It was only after they were married that she saw it dangling down the back of Adam's throat. People said he was brought low long before that day in biology class and there was nothing Maxine could do to save Adam Whitelake from a life spent slithering along the ground. But the wedding vows had been spoken and words like those couldn't be hid under a rock and forgot about. The snake wrapped itself tight around them and called it love but this had nothing to do with passion. This was history pure and simple. All Maxine could do was keep an eye on the snake and make sure that nothing disturbed its peace and hers along with it. She learned to creep softly around the room, especially after Old River (Adam had shed his own name the way a snake sheds its skin) had been drinking. If she went out she was always checking low-hanging branches to make sure she wasn't being watched. At night the snake fell asleep across Maxine's chest and made sure she stayed put. It suffocated her but the more she fought against it the harder it got to breathe.

– I got news, she said. This arrangement's no good.

– Maxine, said Old River, what's important got nothing to do with choice. You can choose what socks to wear in the morning or what to have for dinner. But your name, the person you turn out to be and the people you love are outside of what you can choose. I might have *chosen* to marry someone else but my eyes seen you and nobody else.

– Just my luck, said Maxine.

For all their married life there wasn't a moment that she could turn her back on the snake's needs and look to her own.

A squirrel zigzagged along the counter, stopping every now and then to guzzle down an unattended glass of whiskey before falling asleep in a bowl of pretzels. The bartender kept it for novelty value. As a general rule it nattered cheerfully to customers who, stuporous after a long night of heavy drinking, became convinced that the earth was being invaded by giant rodents from outer space. Every so often the health inspector lodged a formal complaint about having an animal on the premises but did not press the point since the squirrel was significantly cleaner than the people who drank there.

– Where is everybody? demanded Maxine.

The barman jerked his thumb in the direction of the back-room. Maxine pushed her way through a small crowd huddled around the pool table. Most of the Plaza's customers were sports enthusiasts although few of them could walk a straight line. At the table, Fastboy (blind as trust) was hustling a game of pool. Proud of his physique, Fastboy went without a shirt summer and winter. It was as if a giant hand had gripped his pliant body at the joints so that the flesh puffed up on either side. In his youth he had earned a living by lifting heavy objects at funfairs. One day as the crowd pitched pennies at him a man, laughing, shouted:

– Hey, mister! You don't know your own strength.

– No, replied Fastboy, lifting the front end of a Cadillac, but I know my weaknesses.

Now he travelled from city to city working different hustles. People paid good money to see him beat the odds on their behalf. He told Maxine that his father was a bank clerk, a thin man always running, never walking.

– He's probably still running, grinned Fastboy. I haven't seen him since I was six.

Between shots Fastboy laughed loudly and flirted with slack-muscled women in leather jackets. They were always amazed at the apparent ease with which this blind man unfastened even the most complicated undergarment.

– I thought cripples were supposed to sit quiet on street corners, hissed Fastboy's opponent.

He was losing and on his face was the look of a spelling-bee champion suddenly faced with an unfamiliar word. In the quiet of waiting for the next shot to be delivered the air conditioner thumped and snuffled. It gave off an alcohol coolness that evaporated as soon as it touched skin. Circling the table Fastboy waited for instructions from Hatch, his pimple-faced assistant.

– Red ball into right corner pocket, he murmured, positioning the shot.

Maxine caught Fastboy sneaking a look at the opposition from behind his dark glasses. Maxine always suspected that the blindness was a hustle, but it was a point of honour not to give away a man's advantage as long as it cost you nothing. With a casual motion of his wrist Fastboy sent the remaining balls hopping into their holes.

– Don't ever call *me* a fuckin' cripple, he snarled.

Clues fell in small drops from a body that sometimes moved too quickly. It was hard for Fastboy to remember the consequence of every gesture he made.

Money changed hands but nobody walked away rich. Those who had bet on the game and lost sulked until the winners agreed to buy them drinks. A small portion of Fastboy's profit was handed over to Hatch, who scuttled off to meet the woman of his dreams, the waitress at the all-night donut shop. Fastboy packed away his cue and was preparing to leave when he accidentally bumped into Maxine. A good ploy when pretending to be blind.

– You play a good game, Fastboy.

– Maxine? he said. How you tasting tonight?

– Like Boston cream pie, she answered. You seen Old River in here tonight?

Used to trick questions Fastboy replied:

– I *heard* him in here earlier, but the snake was playing up and they turfed him.

Maxine looked up, knife to the point.

– Did you fuck with him?

– What do you think, Maxine? Do I look like a fuckin' snake charmer?

Eight years ago the snake went wild and hurt someone.

54

That was when Old River lost first one job and then another. Sometimes it was that he had a song in his head but the words wouldn't come right. Sometimes it was trying to put a name to a face he'd seen. The snake stopped things from connecting. In the end nobody would hire Old River and he ended up on welfare like almost everybody else in the neighbourhood. For a man whose father had gone from being born to being dead without asking for anybody's help it was bone-scraping humiliation. The woman at the welfare office obviously didn't realize this because she kept asking question after question. Old River never answered any of them. He was too busy trying to keep the boa constrictor quiet. He could feel it uncoiling slow, its head weaving back and forth in that hypnotizing way it had. Old River knew it was having an effect because the woman started looking at him hard through her glasses and asking if he was all right? Did he want a glass of water? It was obvious she knew nothing about snakes or she would have backed off gently without making any sudden moves. But she was stupid and lifted her arm to call someone over. Old River opened his mouth to give warning but the snake slid over his tongue like a peach stone still slimy from the fruit. It wrapped itself around her throat and started to squeeze. There was no denying that as a piece of engineering the snake was an admirable creation: economic, efficient, beautiful. The woman's face was slick with sweat to help it glide down the snake's throat easy. She was turning purple and her hands scrabbled at the coils around her neck but it was no good. Her body had lost about every breath it possessed and the chances of getting any more were looking slim when the boa constrictor loosed its hold and dropped her to the ground. All the people who had suddenly rushed to the woman's aid unnerved the snake. The disadvantage of the slow kill is that there is plenty of room for interruption. A beefy man approached Old River and wrapped a

55

tight piece of cloth around him. It worked the same way as a snake, pinioning his arms so that he couldn't struggle. This is my life, he thought as they dragged him away to the Limestone Psychiatric Hospital. When he came out two years later the snake was so drugged it could barely hiss. A boa constricted.

– I'll tell you something, volunteered Fastboy, Old River has no heart.

– He couldn't live if he had no heart, challenged Maxine.

– He's got a physical heart OK, conceded Fastboy, but there's only craziness where the love should be.

The last ferry to the island blew its horn. The Plaza stood kittycorner to the dock and Fastboy knew that a quick sprint would get him there in time to catch the boat. The island was no more than three miles long and about the same across but it held the entire world for Fastboy. On the other side of the lake lived Rosa the tattooed woman, a sight to give any man pause to think. Her first husband, a tattoo artist, had died in mysterious circumstances, but his artistry was admired by the many lovers she took as consolation. Because Rosa thought Fastboy was a true blind man she described in rich detail the pictures stencilled on her anatomy. Using his naked body as a blank canvas and her finger as a paintbrush, Rosa delicately stroked each body part. Here was a snarling tiger perched on his forearm. A horse galloped along the wall of his chest, the sound of its hooves approximating the beating of his heart. Fastboy blessed the fact that Rosa's husband had been an animal lover. Last, but not least, a rose in full bloom was planted on the inside of his thigh, drawn petal by petal. By the time Rosa finished reciting the entire catalogue, Fastboy was sweating and rickety, a structure threatened with collapse.

– Gotta go, said Fastboy.

– Don't leave me, pleaded Maxine.

Fastboy studied Maxine and mentally weighed the

options. Even without the threat of Old River looming in the background she was no bargain anymore. Worry had strung a thread through the smooth cloth of her face and pulled it tight, leaving her looking closer to fifty than thirty. Desire is a ghost ship and Fastboy was the first to spot a slow leak and jump overboard. He patted her awkwardly on the shoulder.

– You'll find Old River, he said.

– Everyone's leaving me tonight, Maxine complained. I wait and wait and they don't come back. First Old River, then Cowboy and now you.

– Maybe it's your breath, joked Fastboy.

Maxine pressed herself up close so that Fastboy's white cane was wedged painfully between his legs.

– My juice is up, she whispered.

No Rosa tonight, thought Fastboy, only a thorn bush.

– I could tell you a time, confided Maxine, when I wore living colours and *meant* it.

The sky lit up neon blue in those cold and crusty days of early spring. Trees looked spindly without their leaves. Maxine and her younger brother, Joseph, were on their way to the woods behind the deserted farmhouse off Lancashire Road. Joseph had recently lost his first tooth and sent his tongue, a pink periscope, to explore the unfamiliar gap. Like Maxine his hair was black, but wavy with a straight parting down the middle worthy of Moses. Across the bridge of his nose was a smattering of freckles. This gave Joseph an unfinished look, as if his features were only pencilled in. The bulk of his clothing made him appear larger than was true. Layer after layer of winter garments were forced on him by a mother afraid of God, the cold, contagious diseases and almost everything else. The children winced at the chalk-on-blackboard squeak their boots made on the tightly packed snow. Their bodies inclined towards each other in the way of affection before adolescence snatches it, guards it and then throws it away on a perfect stranger. Maxine laid her arm protectively across her brother's shoulders. Along the way Joseph pointed out the various types of birds flying overhead. Crows sitting ugly on the telephone wires were obvious, robins too, but the rest flew incognito as far as Maxine was concerned. The markings that identified one from the other were lost against the sky and the walls where they built their nests.

Colour stains the landscape; it dominates the memory. In school Maxine studied the diaries of Arctic explorers and knew what it was like to be lost in a white maelstrom bereft of maps or common sense. The land sucked the colour out of you and then claimed the body. Shivering at the thought she turned to Joseph.

    — We gotta make a pact, she said.

    — What? he asked.

    — When one of us dies the other has to paint the body in a colour that leaves a mark.

    — Why?

    — We gotta catch God's eye, explained Maxine.

    — Oh, he said.

    — When I get to heaven, declared Maxine, I'm wearing a dress the colour of my own blood.

    — Angels don't wear red, challenged Joseph.

    — This one does.

It was the time of year the Indians called Maple Moon. A week before the spring thaw a local farmer came out to the woods and tapped the sugar maples in preparation for the sap. In exchange for a day's work laboriously boring holes into the wood and inserting the hand-turned spiles through which the sap would drop into waiting buckets, Maxine and Joseph were allowed to come out early and boil down some syrup for themselves. The thaw was only two days old and already the buckets were full waiting to be emptied into a large vat and taken out to the sugar house. Joseph was trying to judge which tree would yield the sweetest sap by counting the number of branches and deciding which one got the sun's warmth first. Maxine's approach was to put her lips to the spile and taste the syrup directly as it came out. Finding one she liked Maxine called out to her brother.

– This one has heart, she announced.

Joseph ignored her and chose a maple a few feet away. Lately Maxine could leave him and stay in one place both at the same time. Earlier their mother had found Maxine in her bedroom, her face covered in lipstick. On her cheek was drawn an extra pair of eyes. Underneath her mouth was an additional nose. There was an ear in the centre of her forehead.

– What are you doing? exclaimed her mother.

– I'm re-inventing myself, Maxine replied.

– I put all my thirty years into inventing you in the first place, argued her mother. I was generous. I left nothing out.

– Yeah yeah yeah, said Maxine.

Now trees had heart. Poetry was a dangerous thing. It wrapped around the tongue like ivy and pretty soon you were left with the ruins of someone who used to talk sense.

– Wood is wood, he admonished. Nothing but.

They collected some of the lower branches, broke them down, and chose a clearing in which to start a small fire. Joseph cupped his chapped hands around the tentative spark and blew puffs of air through the twigs to encourage the blaze. Then they unhooked one of the buckets from the trees and set it on top of the fire. The sap continued to drip from the spile and Maxine watched as the syrup slid like a lascivious hand down the trunk of the tree. It was hard to have something powerful welling up in your body that ached to burst out but was only allowed to trickle. Joseph crouched by the fire to watch the sap boil down and passed the time by whittling a stick, his knife burrowing down into the tender gut.

– Adam Whitelake come asking about you, he said.

– Oh yeah? answered Maxine. What did you say?

– I said I never seen you before in my life.

– Hah hah, said Maxine.

– I bet he eats girls' hearts for breakfast, warned Joseph.

– Indians used to eat the heart of what they killed, said Maxine. They thought it made them brave.

– It don't make Adam Whitelake brave, answered Joseph. Just makes him mean.

– Yeah yeah yeah, said Maxine.

The sap was boiling down. It turned thick and dark. There was a knack to knowing when the syrup was about to burn into sugar crystals and when it was still liquid enough to pour. While Joseph watched over the bucket, Maxine looked around for a patch of clean snow. When she found one, Joseph picked up the bucket and spilled the contents over the ground. The syrup sizzled against the cold and hardened immediately into candy. Joseph picked up a piece and popped it into his mouth.

– How is it? asked Maxine.

– Good, answered Joseph.

The woods were silent except for the occasional sound of sap plop-plopping into the metal buckets. It was the music of spring. Soon the ground would look like an African woman in a torn wedding dress, glimpses of dark earth peeking through the snow. Heavy clothing could be left behind on hooks. Eyelashes weighted down with ice tears would flutter into action. Solemnly Maxine chose a portion of the maple sugar. First she rubbed it against her lips and felt the rough crystal texture. Then she opened her mouth wide and slid the sugar on to her tongue. Her teeth tingled with the excruciating sweetness of it.

– Look, Joseph, she said, I'm eating my own heart.

Thinking about Magritte

The city was built for acrobats. The principal architect, a predecessor of Mr Atkinson, had a love of high-wire acts. So he designed the city to accommodate a famous troupe recently arrived from Italy who liked to keep in practice by leaping from building to building. In order to keep them on their toes the architect threw in the occasional turret or battlement. The craze for replicating the stately homes of Britain was then at its peak. Always there was some spectacular aerial display. Strangers thought the citizens of Limestone incredibly snobbish, their noses constantly in the air. Doctors were kept busy prescribing liniments for stiff necks and bruises which arose from bumping into lamp-posts. Unmarried women took to tying a handkerchief to the chimney for the pleasure of seeing their favourite acrobat bounding through the air, a piece of fragile silk clenched suggestively in his teeth. Only once was there an accident. The oldest member of the troupe, too vain to wear glasses, miscalculated the distance between two rooftops and fell, feet first, into a pair of man's longjohns hanging out on a washline to dry. There he was suspended, bouncing helpless as a baby, until the firemen came and cut him down.

– That was the only time, boasted Gonzino Bay, my ancestors ever worked with a net.

On the roof of the Plaza Hotel a company of acrobats, descendants of the original, rehearsed a human pyramid.

Bearing the weight on the bottom row were three thick-armed youths and their father, Gonzino Bay. There was a fourth son but his near-sightedness (an inherited weakness) proved an insurmountable handicap. After dropping his sister three times he was forced to retire and became a librarian. In his own youth Gonzino Bay enjoyed a passing resemblance to Victor Mature. Before it passed completely his wife Alice had married him. The elegance of her neck used to excite him so much that one night he ejaculated thirty-five feet above ground. By the time he had finished performing the double somersault-with-a-half-twist, climbed down from the platform and taken a bow the semen had dried in a sequinned patch on his leotard.

But that was thirty years ago. Gonzino Bay's body ached under the weight of his responsibilities. The youngest boy needed dental work. Audiences were smaller and more cynical. They carried the thrill of flying unaided in small vials of pills. These things were a sulking giant on his back. He felt Alice's toe (God bless it!) digging into his spine and tried shifting to a more comfortable position. Soon the family would have to climb down from his shoulders and offer him theirs. Not far away a single light shone from a window. Gonzino Bay wondered if the person behind the glass knew he was being watched by a man whose job was to fly through the air catching his family one by one before they fell hard to the ground.

★   ★   ★

Ernie swore that he would never touch another drop of tequila as long as he lived. For the past hour he felt as though he was being watched by a troupe of second-rate acrobats. When at last he fell asleep his dreams were of Orville and Wilbur Wright. They wore orange silk pyjamas. Their shoes were made of grass.

63

Dixie Chicken

Libra's was the one restaurant in Limestone that stayed open all night. The only reservations you needed were those you brought with you about eating there in the first place. It catered for the truck drivers, musicians and drunks who rambled in from off the street or the Plaza a few blocks south. The restaurant had stood on the same spot on lower Divide Street for decades. For entertainment value it rivalled the Theatre Royal next door. (Unlike Libra's, that establishment had briefly closed its doors when a production of Molière's *The Miser*, performed by the officers of the local garrison, was halted by the church. The *Limestone Gazette* noted, however, that Staff Sergeant Vickers had attacked the role of Frosine with "wit and dash".) The decor of Libra's consisted of murals depicting the Italian countryside which, if they'd been exhibited to the public at large, might have killed the Italian tourist industry stone dead. Waitresses with connect-the-dot eyebrows, lacquered hair and ortho-paedic shoes performed a dance peculiar to Libra's. One hand went up, balancing a tray, while the other removed an unwanted arm from around the waist. The bottom swung around to avoid being pinched while the feet skilfully stomped on the cockroaches scuttling brazenly across the floor. Patrons called it the Libra shuffle.

It was a busy night. The cook threatened to quit every five minutes as he'd done for the last twenty-three years. Orders were mixed up or forgotten altogether but it didn't matter since nobody came for the food. At one of the booths sat a woman wearing an ill-fitting wig. Across the aisle was a musician, a thin and wild-eyed boy. He hailed from the deep south where music lay in the ground just waiting to be harvested.

– You are delicate as spun sugar, thought Doris, licking her lips.

She couldn't help imagining him on top of her as he crumbled into fine powder. Each grain a sweet testament on her skin.

– Oh goody, she whispered.

Bored and restless the boy brought out his guitar. Solemn as a marriage vow he slipped a piece of hollowed bone over his ring finger and slid it slowly down the fret. The bone collected notes as it went along and when it reached the mouth of the guitar released a honey metal sound. This music possessed the boy with a sense of serious purpose. It was an archive of sounds and smells, a way of life. It was part of a pattern as old as movement. From now on he had a new motto.

– So long, baby, he sang, it's been good to know you.

The Midnight Cowboy noticed Doris sitting at a booth nursing a cup of coffee. Reaching the table he offered a smile that was dog-friendly.

– Hey, Doris! he said.

– Cowboy, she answered. Have a seat.

– You alone? he enquired.

– More and more, she sighed.

The flourescent lighting overhead picked out the grainy wrinkles which lined Doris' face. It showed up the sagging jowls and the crinkled skin of her cleavage. Untold men had buried their heads in Doris' bosom, but that was an old story now. There seemed an impossible distance between the young woman Cowboy remembered and this woman in the droopy years of middle life. And no bridge to get him safe to the other side. Cowboy slid into the booth. His damp clothing stuck to the seat and plucked at his skin as he tried to find a comfortable position.

– I saw Mrs Munscher tonight, confided Cowboy.

– Oh yeah? said Doris, narrowing her eyes. What were you doing at the Rainbow House of Beauty?

– Looking for Lily, he admitted.

– You gotta stop hanging around with dead people, observed Doris, they got a cold view of the world.

On the back wall of the restaurant was a painting of a Tuscan village. The houses were tall and crooked with long green shutters locked tight against the curious eyes of the neighbours. Because the artist worked all day as an insurance agent the village was painted in twilight amid the stars and a half moon modelled on a Romano cheese left over from the artist's supper. Suspended indefinitely above the roofs of the village was an acrobat. Defying the laws of both gravity and common sense, the man's neck was curved backwards, his gaze directed towards the stars, trusting his body to take him safely back home. The acrobat carried the pale moon on his back.

– You look terrible, Cowboy, said Doris.

– Lily keeps swimming around with the fish in my head, said Cowboy.

– I miss her too, Doris pointed out. She was my best friend.

– I know, sighed Cowboy.

A young waitress broke with tradition and did the cancan past their table, disappearing into the kitchen.

– Do you know how you got your name? asked Doris.

Cowboy shook his head. Not because he hadn't heard the story a hundred times but because he knew that Doris, proud of her part, loved the telling.

– I was with Lily the night you was born, she began.

A whole day and night Lily was in labour but she never complained. Then you finally come. I'd never seen a baby born fresh like that. Frankly, Cowboy, I was worried. You looked all sick and weak with that twisted leg and your forehead all puffed up. And there was blood everywhere. It's a true thing that people are careless with what keeps them alive. But Lily just held you close and said to me: Born at midnight to a world that's against him. My Midnight Cowboy. Personally, I wanted to call you Rodney.

– I want proof that Lily didn't want to leave me, sniffed Cowboy.

– People love you and leave you, declared Doris. That's what they do. I'm going for a donut.

Planting a kiss on top of Cowboy's head, Doris left him. At the door she ran into Frank and Savage. Squatting so that her face was level with Frank's stomach, Doris poked a cautious finger in the direction of his belly button.

– Hello, junior, she gurgled. How's it going Frank?

– I'm good, said Frank, but the baby's quiet.

– Be thankful, said Doris. Once they're born, man and boy, they give you no peace.

– You look nice tonight, remarked Savage.

– Tell it to the marines, she giggled, straightening her wig.

Savage settled in with Cowboy and motioned Frank to do the same. A waitress joined them and all three could tell from the bruises and the straight way she walked that she was new to Libra's. Her name tag indicated that she was called Graciella but Frank never believed anything he read.

– What'll you have? she asked.

– French fries and gravy, ordered Savage in a whisper, and coffee.

– What? demanded Graciella.

– FRENCH FRIES, GRAVY AND COFFEE! shouted Savage.

67

– And a glass of milk for the baby, added Frank.

Making a mental note never to work the Gondolier section again, Graciella left to fill their order.

– Tough night, Cowboy? asked Frank.

– Maxine sent me out lookin' for Old River but I haven't found him yet. I thought maybe he'd be here but he isn't.

A low whistle sounded on the other side of the table. It was common knowledge that Old River had a crawling king snake in his head. When it got mad it was like cutting into lemons. The stinging juice of it hit you straight in the eye. Looking for the man was one thing but actually finding him was another.

– Maxine been rattling your bones? asked Savage.

Cowboy nodded his head. Pity sat up straight in Savage.

– You're hills and valleys, Cowboy, he said. People walk all over you.

Graciella returned and slung the coffee onto the table.

– She learns fast, commented Frank.

Liquid sloshed over the side of the cup, staining the denture whiteness of it. Frank pulled it towards him and cautiously slurped the hot coffee. From the kitchen came the sharp sound of broken crockery, followed by fluent Italian.

– Listen, said Frank, sensing tension all around him. I'll draw you a story.

Once he had known a kid everyone called Norman the Fat Boy. They met at university during a time when the voices in Frank's head were silent.

– It shows, Frank pointed out, that I've been liking institutions all my life.

The professor, who among other things had taught them how to make licence plates, invited a famous literary critic to present a lecture. The man claimed to have detected a singular pattern which applied to every work of literature. The critic had expounded his theory in classrooms and lecture halls from Tokyo to Timbuctoo so that students around the world now looked at literature in terms of answers rather than questions. Because of this the critic was surprised at the end of his talk when a hand was raised.

– Yes? he demanded.

Realizing that it was Norman the Fat Boy, the class rolled their eyes. In those days he was considered the lunatic.

– What do you do, asked Norman, when you know everything there is to know in the world?

Nobody uttered a sound. The professor gulped and the critic blinked.

– I suppose, he said lamely, on the seventh day you rest. Hah hah hah.

– I see, replied Norman quietly.

The next day they found Norman the Fat Boy hanging by a rope from his bedroom ceiling. He left no written message behind.

– The point of the story, concluded Frank, because he knew one was expected of him, is that not everything in this world fits a pattern.

Fresh customers stood in line waiting impatiently for booths to empty. The management bustled from table to table encouraging people to eat quickly and leave. They were happy to oblige – it wasn't cuisine to linger over. Already Graciella was pirouetting over to Cowboy's table with the bill. As she slapped it down, Frank lightly touched her wrist.

– I'm going to have a baby, he said.

– I'm not looking for crazy, she barked.

Like the outline of a hand slapped onto rising dough, the imprint of that remark remained on Frank's face. Both Cowboy and Savage, noting Frank's stricken expression, tried to say something reassuring but found themselves unable to speak. Grease from the meal coated their mouths so that words slid around without taking hold.

– Offer people a thought sweet as pie, thought Frank with regret, and they throw it right back in your face.

All around them was the sound of spaghetti being sucked off the plate. The rattle and clap of conversation. Frank felt a sense of panic rising in him. It nipped at the heels of his dearest thoughts and made them scatter. He thought about having to return to the hospital where his whole life was documented on little white cards but there was nobody who knew him the way Savage and Cowboy did. On his first visit to the Limestone Psychiatric Hospital his father, Oswald, had held his hand as they looked at the imposing structure.

– I know nothing about the human mind, said Oswald, but I know roads. I've built hundreds and not one of them was completely straight. It didn't stop anyone from getting to where they wanted to go.

Next to the hospital was an amusement park. The two properties were separated by a chain-link fence through which the patients watched the summer festivities. It intrigued Frank to see families paying for the privilege of experiencing the way the patients of the Limestone Psychiatric Hospital lived for free. They disoriented themselves in violent rides which swung high and then swooped low to the ground. A hall of mirrors distorted common objects and made them appear frightening. In the short, dark passage of the Chamber of Horrors men and women succumbed to their imagination and began to view the world as suspect and frightening. But the ride which commanded Frank's complete attention was the roller-coaster. It was painted to look like a dragon. The front car was the head of the monster. A stream of orange flames shot out of its nostrils. The other cars made up the body. They were painted green with criss-crosses of metallic paint. Its feet were tucked underneath the belly which gave the impression, once the ride was at full speed, that the dragon was in flight. As

70

people took their seats the attendant walked the length of the cars securing the safety bars. They made a heavy clunk as they locked into place, like prison cells shutting one after another, signalling a point of no return. Sensing this, one girl screamed for release. But the cars jerked forward and her screams were absorbed by the others that joined it. The dragon creaked slowly along the track until it reached the crest of the first loop. There it paused as though to catch its breath. The riders released their grips on the safety bars and in a moment of bravado waved to their friends on the ground. Then with dizzying speed the roller-coaster plunged into space. The dragon dipped and raced as if in pursuit. The cars slanted dangerously to the side, delighting the young men whose girlfriends were compelled to lean heavily against them. When the cars reached the top of the third loop the track twisted around completely so that for a brief, exhilarating moment the dragon flew upside down. Here was a toy invented by a man in love with gravity, a man more concerned with the justice than the laws of nature. Frank related this incident to his father when he came to visit.

– The people look like they should fall out but they don't, exclaimed Frank.

– It's specially built so they don't fall out, explained Oswald.

Wetting the corner of a napkin with his tongue, Savage wiped away some gravy that had dribbled onto Frank's beard during the meal.

– OK, Frank?

– I'm upside down, answered Frank, but the baby's safe. Monsters are harmless when you know their tricks.

Baroque Convertible

Revellers made slow progress home from the Plaza. Like a marble tossed into a basin they travelled in noisy circular motions. In this tangle of side streets surrounding the hotel were houses belonging to Limestone's Italian community. Their verandas were strung with green paper lanterns, remnants of a recent religious festival. Wives peered angrily through white lace curtains as their husbands tiptoed through rock gardens patterned in the shape of a saint. They tried not to dislodge a nose or a halo. Exhausted, the men settled into a clattering stillness at their doorstep. Until dawn the women would lecture them. They used arguments as strong as cast-iron skillets and as delicate as the legs of a spider. Clothes that had been lovingly washed and ironed that morning were tossed into the street. Both parties prayed to the Virgin Mary as their daughters, grateful for the diversion, snuck out the bedroom window to meet their lovers in the bushes.

This was every-night drama. Cowboy limped through these streets in the company of Frank and Savage, bowing to the women, winking at the men and all the time dodging flying nightshirts and suspender belts. Men and women got the juice up on each other and squeezed themselves dry. In an hour or two the husbands would start to feel amorous and search for a quiet space in the women's anger. With the ease of long practice they inserted the moon and a flattering comparison with their wives' thighs. After that the only sound was of couples unfurling their limbs and testing the true depth of their affection for each other.

The night had reached its darkest point. It was a blanket under which all sorts of suspect transactions could be effected in secrecy. Cowboy was glad of Frank's company. A man used to defying the laws of nature was a valued friend to a cripple. He reached out and grabbed a corner of Frank's shirt tail, which was stiff with dried food and bicycle grease. It was like a child's geography project. The numerous textures and stains represented all the various terrains he'd travelled.

– I like to know where I stand, asserted Frank.

The trio advanced on the Plaza Hotel like gunfighters in a Western.

– This is what Lily meant, thought Cowboy, when she give me my name.

In the north end laws were fashioned to suit the purpose of the strong. Threats of violence shot like arrows from behind empty buildings and parked cars. Legendary gunfighters didn't roam the streets, but Cowboy would sooner have met up with Billy the Kid than Old River in a bad mood. Shadowy corners and the moon, a faraway light, offered little protection to the man whose only weapon was an affectionate heart.

– Hey, Frank? ventured Cowboy.

– Yeah?

– If the baby's a girl you could name it Lily, he suggested.

– Babies need a clean start, replied Frank.

– That's what I'm saying, answered Cowboy. Lilies are clean.

– They're for the dead, Cowboy, sighed Frank.

From out of the gloom drifted the plumed notes of a harmonica.

– What's that? demanded Savage.

– It's Hatch, answered Frank.

Standing outside the donut shop was Fastboy's lovelorn assistant. In preparation for his tryst with Moonie, his beloved waitress, Hatch had adorned himself with a bow tie that lit up in the dark and a top hat with the top missing. He was pacing back and forth in the shadows trying to work up the courage to enter the shop. After clearing his throat and hefting a wad of spit into the gutter, Hatch blew the opening bars to "Do Not Forsake Me, Oh My Darling". He looked over at Cowboy.

– You got trouble, he snorted.
– You come from the Plaza? asked Cowboy.
– Yeah, said Hatch.
– Is Old River there? asked Savage.

Hatch stood on tiptoe. He measured five feet high, a bare inch over Savage, and was always trying to use this to his advantage. He never succeeded.

– No, he mumbled, but Maxine's waiting.
– Does she look mad? asked Cowboy anxiously.
– Every time I see her, replied Hatch.
– Where you going? asked Frank.
– I'm going to howl at the Moonie.
– She don't know you're alive, scoffed Savage.
– True, admitted Hatch, but I love her flat feet.
– Good luck, said Frank.

The door to the Plaza bar was unlocked so they walked inside. The only two people left besides the barman were Fastboy (blind as love) and Maxine. They were feeding olives to the squirrel. Maxine swivelled around on the bar stool.

– I been waiting, Cowboy, she said.
– I've been lookin' everywhere, he answered.
– So where's Old River?

74

The question landed quiet and dangerous. A cat with its claws out.

– I don't know, he admitted.

Unbuckling her voice Maxine let him have it, whack!, across the face.

– Some detective you are! she yelled. Some fuckin' detective!

Her anger was a fly buzzing loud in their ears. The barman lowered his head behind the counter and counted his stock of maraschino cherries for the second time that night. Only Savage was unperturbed. It was his job to smooth ruffled feathers.

– Hey, Maxine, he cooed, Old River's probably out with the dogs.

She glared at this cool little kid. White as a scoop of vanilla ice cream and so thin one good licking would finish him off.

– You think so? she said, and then, OK, who's gonna come with me?

Maxine had a terror of dogs. Even the ones no bigger than a teacup threw her into a panic. There was a V-shaped scar in the corner of her left eye. On a bad day Maxine could still feel the dog's teeth digging for soft white bone. It gave her face a look sometimes like James Cagney doing his famous snarl. The scar was a reminder that everything she felt had something physical to go with it. Inside and outside worked together in Maxine.

– Who's coming with me? she repeated. Cowboy?

Frankly, he was sick of searching for things that weren't his own. Old River would yell at him or worse for showing up at the dogs. One time before Cowboy had travelled out to the kennels to collect Old River. Everybody had a different idea about what he did out there but they guessed it was women. It was a warm animal place and Maxine was almost sure not to follow. When Cowboy arrived the place was dark and silent. The doorway was scored with knife marks. It was a trick of Old River's to make a notch in the entrance to a place. The door of No. 22 Colbourne Street had to be replaced three times since Old River's arrival.

– Make the first cut, Cowboy, he declared, and chances are you come away safe.

Keeping in mind what people said about the women Cowboy kept away from the kennels. Safer to be in the eye of a hurricane than to spy on Old River. But Maxine was giving no option, he knew that. If he refused to go with her she'd cut him the way Old River did a door. Maxine made sure that other people showed the marks of her pain. Cowboy resigned himself to his fate.

– I'll come with you, he said.

It was a sad fact of this world that you had to move through what you hated most to get to what you loved best.

Profiterole Bongo

T he donut (pink, wet and decadent) lay against its brethern. Here was an orgy of multicoloured pastries. Dark chocolate, honey-glazed and raspberry centres. Day and night pastry chefs laboured to invent new types of donuts for their customers' pleasure. They experimented with fillings, toppings, colours and tastes. There were seasonal donuts for Christmas and St Patrick's Day. Staring at the fifty different kinds on offer Doris was overwhelmed by the possibilities. It made her loony as a beetle.

Aside from Moonie, the waitress, Doris was the only living soul in the place. She had found Moonie, red hair flying in sparks from her head, sawing relentlessly on a violin. Eager to promote new talent, Doris good-naturedly played the conductor. This was done with such a boisterous rocking of the body and waving of arms that Moonie began to feel seasick and temporarily abandoned her musicianship.

– It's a quarter to three, sang Doris. And no one in the place except you and me.

– It's past three o'clock already, Doris.

– Poetic licence, she said. How ya doin', Moonie?

– Ridin' easy. How's yourself?

– I've lost my black-eyed soul boy, sighed Doris.

Moonie clucked her tongue and pointed to the shelves behind her.

– I'm surrounded by sweet and tender things, she said, but they don't break my heart.

77

– Nice work if you can get it, agreed Doris. Where'd you get the violin?

– Ernie give it to me tonight.

– Don't play it around cats, cautioned Doris.

– You see any cats here? demanded Moonie. You come in for a donut or not?

– I'm looking.

Doris commenced the evening ritual of walking back and forth in front of the counter. Methodically she examined each donut, trying to figure out which one would satisfy her craving. Moonie stood, plate at the ready, to retrieve the chosen pastry. But this was the highlight of Doris' day and the decision would not be rushed. Finally the pacing stopped.

– The Coconut Glacier tonight please, Moonie, she said.

– You sure, Doris? questioned Moonie. I can't tempt you with the Chocolate Rum or maybe a Cherry Twist?

Doris remained firm. She spread her legs, tilted her head a little to one side and in a voice that was mock-gangster tough commanded Moonie to:

– Hand over the dough.

Moonie placed the donut on the plate and returned to her violin. She positioned the instrument firmly under one of her chins.

It was a surprise to see Sam walk through the door.

– Hello, Doris, he said.

– Hello, she said. I thought you were dead.

He ran his tongue along her cheek. His spit smelled of whiskey but she didn't move. When somebody offers proof of their existence you can't wipe it away.

– How are things? asked Doris.

Sam brought his face close to hers.

– What am I thinking right now? he asked.

78

– You are thinking of being a cowboy. Your hands are blistered. You have dust in your mouth.

– Well, he said, you're right.

That's how things stood with Sam and Doris. Their life together was a hurly-burly. Sam threw words like a lasso, jerking Doris close to him and then letting her go. Doris always knew when the rope was going to fall and didn't bother trying to run anymore. She stayed in range.

– What are you doing here? he asked.

– I'm waiting for my lucky break to come along, she whispered confidentially. I spend a lot of time this way.

– That's you all over, he said. Waiting waiting waiting.

– Mostly for you, Sam. Almost always for you. Certainly that's how I spent 1963.

– We had a good marriage, Doris, he sighed.

– We shared windows and doors.

Still hovering outside the donut shop, face pressed to the glass, was Hatch. He gazed adoringly as Moonie busily stuffed a Chocolate Cream Horn into her mouth, a dented cupid's bow. She looked like an angel. A seraph in an orange polyester uniform. Illuminating his bow tie, Hatch stepped over the threshold and sidled up to Moonie.

– You want somethin'? she asked.

Clambering onto one of the counter stools, Hatch signalled her to come closer. His breath smelled of pickled herrings.

– I French-kissed a chicken once, he said, sticking out his tongue, and I got the scars to prove it.

– Romance is dead, thought Moonie.

Sam was staring hard at Doris. His eyes took in the wig perched like an exhausted turtle on top of her skull, the knobby fingers picking nervously at her donut.

– You haven't aged so well as I thought you would, he said.

– You think I'm a prisoner of one design? challenged Doris. You were never generous.

With one finger Sam casually traced the words "fuck you" which someone had scratched onto the table.

– What I remember about our wedding, he continued, is that we had peas with our dinner. I hate peas. It ruined the whole day for me.

Doris ignored this remark.

– On our first night together, she reminisced, I sat up for hours just to listen to your breathing. I loved the way your chest rose and fell in such *beautiful* rhythms.

– Jesus! groaned Sam. That's why I left. I couldn't forgive you for watching me so closely.

Noting the violin propped against the coffee machine, Hatch brought out his harmonica.

– You like music, Moonie? he asked.

– It was a present, she said.

– Have I got a rival? cried Hatch, clutching at his heart and tumbling backwards off the stool.

– You're not even in the running, declared Moonie.

The shadow of lovers.

– Evening, Hatch! called Doris.

– Hey, Doris, he murmured.

– Do you know "Shine on Harvest Moon"? queried Sam.

The only requests Hatch ever got were to bugger off.

– I think so, he answered.

Sam hoisted himself out of his seat and offered a hand to Doris.

– May I have the honour?

Pleased as a schoolgirl Doris allowed herself to be sucked into the arms of a man who refused to believe that romance was solely a young man's game. It didn't matter that Sam's hair was now as thin as his excuses. She lay her cheek against the crêpe-like skin of his neck and made no comparisons.

> The night was mighty dark
> So you could hardly see
> 'Cause the moon refused to shine.

The couple clung to each other and remembered vividly, without sadness, a time when hip against hip seemed the most natural position in the world. When the song ended they remained standing, swaying slightly from the exertion. Sam bit Doris lightly on the nose.

– We should have had children, she ventured. I would have had somewhere to put my memories of you.

– I don't owe you another life, he whispered.

Hatch cleared his throat. Sam had forgotten the cost of making poetic gestures and dug reluctantly into his pocket. He fished out a small coin.

– Never walk away empty-handed, Fastboy had taught him.

– Thanks, muttered Hatch, accepting the money.

– Give the man a Pineapple Jelly! cried Doris. That's one of the best kinds.

Sam was gathering his belongings.

– You're not going? she asked.

– I can't stay, he replied.

Doris drew a sharp breath.

– I have cancer, she said.

– Shit, he said and paused, really?

– No, she relented, I was only planting a new flag on old territory.

Sam smiled and took Doris' head in his hands. He pressed it gently against his stomach.

– I can hear the music of what makes you work, she sighed.

– What am I thinking right now? he asked.

– You are thinking of being a priest. Your hands are soft and white. There is wine on your lips.

– Well, he said, you are right.

And with a wave and a walk he was gone.

Ocean Run into the Sea

High above the pavement Gonzino Bay tiptoed among the flower boxes and swung out onto flagpoles. Even sleepwalking he preferred the spaces where angels dangled their toes.

– What are you looking at, Cowboy? asked Maxine.

– Acrobats, he answered.

– Oh yeah?

– Ernie says I'll be an angel when I die, smiled Cowboy. I can look out for you then.

– You'll be an angel fish more like, snorted Maxine.

– I'm a mermaid, sighed Cowboy, I'm the best kind of fish.

Across the top of billboards advertising deluxe cars and better-behaved children Gonzino Bay laid out the different costumes he wore each night. Real diamonds were sewn into the collars. The material was the colour of oceans. It was Gonzino Bay's idea that as he and his family floated from pole to pole the audience should look up and see waves.

– Turn the world upside down, said Gonzino Bay to Alice, it's what they pay to see.

Children left the arena thinking of raindrops as fallen acrobats.

Duke Street extended from one end of the city's fortunes to the other, like the arm of a starving musician who, in his fist, clutches a bouquet of flowers. It ran parallel to the waterfront. Maxine and Cowboy headed in the opposite direction to Independence Park and the manicured lakeside properties which made Limestone a favourite vacation spot. They followed the dark glass edge of the lake and ignored the picturesque harbour where the visitors' sailboats were anchored for the night. The masts knocked against each other like bones. The history of Limestone was written on the water. Between the shipping lines, which had carried to these shores settlers, grain and the steadfast religions, were later boats bringing immigrants, music and cholera. Unable to find housing, the sick were left to their own devices. They lived in hastily constructed shanties on the docks. A yellow flag was raised in warning to passing ships. Doctors experimented with the efficacy of various elixirs as a preventative medicine. The most popular was brandy. The minister of Health and Sanitation, possessing a practical temperament, blamed the epidemic on the pigs which were allowed to roam the streets at will. Those of a more religious persuasion were convinced that the cholera was a sign of God's displeasure. Days of public humiliation and prayer were proclaimed and taverns were converted into makeshift churches. (The Plaza refused and lost not one customer to the disease.) Meanwhile the afflicted died in their hundreds. They were lowered into a common grave and sank without trace.

The last bus Maxine had taken was the one that brought her and Old River to Limestone fifteen years ago. Only one ran at this time of night. The driver was an insomniac who had persuaded the bus company to offer a graveyard shift service. A computerized map indicated where the highest proportion of paying customers were likely to be found. Unwilling to follow such a narrowly proscribed route the driver conducted an arbitrary tour of Limestone. He

shuffled landmarks and neighbourhoods so that nobody was
entirely confident of where they belonged. Sharp lines of
daylight behaviour were blurred. The bus rambled through
the north end, turning down side streets to collect passengers who might want a midnight swim or to visit a relative.
Children hosted overnight parties, huddled under Mickey
Mouse blankets while the driver told them ghost stories,
creeping the bus past the cemetery for effect. Claustro-
phobics were allowed to ride on top of the bus. Cutting
across Divide Street the driver reached the university cam-
pus where students celebrating a football victory draped
the bus in the school colours. On quiet nights the driver
concentrated on learning Chinese from a Berlitz language
tape. Maxine wondered how much it cost to ride on a bus
now and whether she needed exact change. Tonight this
kind of problem seemed insurmountable and she turned to
Cowboy.

    – Let's walk, she said.

    – I'm no good for that distance, Maxine, he answered.

    – You can kiss me, she offered.

    A mass of tiny fish collected in Cowboy's nostrils. Wrig-
gling in anticipation they caused him to sneeze. They
smudged the purity of the moment.

    – You want to kiss me or what? demanded Maxine.

    – Is this a gift? breathed Cowboy.

    – I'm waiting, she replied.

    Cowboy limped towards her.

    – Walk to me level, she snapped. You're making me
dizzy.

    He came closer and closer. He wanted to see how close
desire could come without breaking down. A compilation
of all the great Hollywood kisses flashed through his mind
as he manoeuvred into the correct position. He wondered
whether it was too late to moisten his lips. Just as Cowboy
was about to plant his kiss, Maxine grabbed the collar of

her shirt and pulled it over her face. Cowboy had no time to pull back. His once-in-a-lifetime kiss landed on a mouth protected by 100 percent polyester.

– I don't want to catch anything, she said.

Cowboy didn't know what to do next. Fortunately (this was true Hollywood) the bus arrived. Suddenly there seemed to Cowboy something friendly and honest about a machine. With a bus you knew your ultimate destination. All you had to do was sit and wait until you got there. If there was supposed to be a kiss at the end of the road then there'd be a kiss. Human beings, on the other hand, turned without warning on to treacherous roads. They abandoned you in the mud. They threw synthetic fibres between a man and his passion. Cowboy boarded the bus.

– 八十五 仙, said the driver.

– What? asked Cowboy.

– Eighty-five cents.

Cowboy paid the fare and fell into a seat at the back. Maxine followed.

– You can't put your faith in a machine, she said loudly. It might break down in a lonely place.

From his roof-top perch Gonzino Bay waved goodbye.

– C'mon, let's go! Let's go! Let's fuckin' *go*!

The only other passenger was a man who grabbed the bar of the seat in front of him and rocked against it as if he could propel the bus forward through sheer force of will. The man was stumbling through a jungle. The kind with tables, chairs and a coffee pot. One filled with kids whose veins glowed through pale skin mapping out their life expectancy.

– I know how you feel, thought Maxine.

Buses never went fast enough or took you as far as you wanted to go.

★

Scratch the surface and blood comes running. It was the fall of Maxine's sixteenth year, a time that made you look to the ground. Thick piles of leaves sinking into wet earth and Maxine sinking along with them. She and Adam Whitelake lay in the clearing behind the deserted farmhouse. There he wooed her with seasons.

– Summer is wet kisses on the inside of your skin, he said.

One by one Adam undid the buttons of her blouse.

– You are beautiful, he murmured.

With a single word Adam ripped off the skin that protected her heart. Still, Maxine knew it was a bribe. They both did. But in this foreign country of sweat and kisses she was forced to accept whatever currency was offered. Slipping her hand underneath his sweater Maxine felt Adam's ribs. They spread upwards like the bow of an old-fashioned ship.

– Tell me spring, she whispered.

– That's kittens, he said, jumping at the sight of their own shadow.

A light breeze blew through the trees. Leaves twitched on the ground. With the concentration of a child playing toy soldiers, Adam positioned her limbs. His hands were calloused from driving his grandfather's tractor after school but Maxine was grateful for his guidance. This was her first time and she was unsure of what part she was supposed to play. Maxine caught a whiff of peppermint as Adam writhed on top of her. She never expected a clean smell like that from such a grubby boy. Sweat rounded off their noses, cheeks, breasts, hips. The angles of their bodies melted into each other. In Adam's eyes Maxine saw a reflection of herself. A prisoner of his way of seeing things. They were snake eyes and no mistake. They sank into her own and held her fast. A quick dry tongue flickered against her cheek. It was a sign of terrifying affection.

– OK, gasped Maxine, what's winter?

– Winter's a giant tongue, whispered Adam, that licks all the colour away.

Love is a fast and burning thing. It came to Maxine under maple trees dyed red with the kisses of a thousand women.

– Was it sweet? he asked.

– Molasses pouring from mouth to mouth, she answered.

Sometimes a pinprick is all it takes to shaft a heart and fill the street with blood.

– I've wrapped my arms around a dead man tonight, Cowboy, said Maxine. Let's get off the bus.

Bayou Gumbo

The dogs were kept three miles from the city, beyond the bus depot and behind a newly built fast-food restaurant. The shelter was a squat building of concrete and wire with an enclosed run out back where the dogs were exercised. In the spring, after the snows melted, the ground was dotted with perfectly preserved mounds of dog shit. Animals found scrounging among the city's landscaped gardens were dumped here along with a generous cheque for the charity that ran the place. After three weeks and one sad-eyed photo in the *Limestone Gazette*, the unwanted animal was killed. Rumours circulated about where the fast-food restaurant got its meat.

Not all the dogs had four legs. Old River could be found regularly banging on the door. It was usually a late visit so that by the time he got home Maxine was a hot coal that burned him, then warmed him and then lay cold in his bed. The night guard shed copious tears every time a dog was put to sleep. He eyed Old River with suspicion.

– Why you want to see the dogs? he asked.

– I'm looking for my long-lost pet, answered Old River. It was stolen by gypsies.

– Yeah? What does it look like?

– It's got four legs, a tail and a patch over one eye.

– Which eye? demanded the guard.

– The left one, replied Old River.

– Got no dogs answering to that description, said the guard.

– Maybe they changed the license plates, suggested Old River.

Since the guard was a sentimental man he allowed himself to be bribed with a mickey of rum.

The first room was set aside for cats. It was divided by a long corridor, on either side of which were wire cages, double stacked. The floor was sticky with a combination of antiseptic and detergent. Clumps of stray fur nested in the corners. Old River hated cats.

– Fuckin' useless animals, he hissed.

His grandmother had owned a cat who refused to shit in a litter box. Instead it chose cunning places which were difficult to locate and hard to clean. It was Old River's job when he came to visit to find and dispose of the mess. He loathed the self-satisfied look on the cat's face. Maxine grunted when he complained.

– You and that cat are just the same, she said. You leave behind all kinds of shit and expect me to clean it up.

In one cage three black cats clustered around a saucer of milk like mourners weeping over a corpse.

Every man needs a patch of ground where he is king. It goes right down the line until you come to the men who preside over nothing more than a bowling alley on Saturday night. For Old River it was the kennels. It wasn't No. 22 Colbourne Street, that's for damn sure. Marriage had proved a slippery thing and Old River was never able to grasp it. Like a snake, but not so much as people thought. The snake in his head followed the rules of nature and once you'd figured them out you could live with the consequences. There was no real mystery to a snake. But Maxine was wriggling out of his embrace and there were no guidelines to getting her back. When they were young Old River had admired her coarse beauty above everything. When you rubbed up against Maxine you really *felt* something. Now what he felt was that he was a constant disappointment.

Old River moved towards the dogs. What he required was a powerful noise. A deep-throated howl. The lights were low so he couldn't tell how many dogs were being kept in the kennels. Old River switched on the lights to full and stepped into the middle of the room. He raised his arms and waited. For a second there was no movement from the cages. The dogs were startled out of sleep but when they saw Old River they began hurling themselves at the wire. They wanted to throw themselves at his feet. It didn't seem to matter how badly a dog was treated, kick its ass and the animal still crawled back for love. It wasn't a quality Old River admired but he used it to his advantage. The dogs were like fans screaming for their favourite singer. They whimpered and barked but Old River only heard applause. Who was he tonight? Not Elvis Presley, that queer boy in a white sequinned suit. This time he was playing Gene Vincent. Pock marks and greasy hair, the kind of ugliness a man could carry if he moved his hips the right way. The hanging light made the shape of a crescent moon on the curve of Old River's forearm.

– I'll give you the moon, he promised.

He held out the tips of his fingers to his hysterical admirers. That's how Maxine was in the early days. She panted for attention, her tongue hanging out. He was still called Adam Whitelake then with all the advantages of being the first man in her life. But the snake was there too, coiled around his brain and waiting. Sometimes it squeezed out comments guaranteed to break a young girl into a thousand pieces and the penitent kisses would have to come quick. After a time he got smart and realized that the snake had to be kept occupied. So he fed it scraps of what Maxine looked like: blue inkstains on her fingers, the fleshy pink underlip. She was a kaleidoscope of liquid colours moving against the sheets. He'd longed to tell Maxine about the thousand ways of moving that she had, the way they cut into his heart. Like the way instead of saying prayers at night she blew kisses to the people that she loved. Or the way she tugged on her earlobe when she was nervous. But Maxine was a self-conscious woman and she'd have tried to make those gestures perfect. So he decided to keep quiet. He thought about telling Maxine he loved her. But he never did. With the warm breath of the animals still on him, Old River went home. He always fucked Maxine better after he'd seen the dogs.

Remembrance of a Journey

S tanding guard over the waterfront was Limestone's unofficial mascot, a black cast-iron sculpture of a lion. Curled up underneath it was a man asleep. On his head was a bowler hat. In his clenched fist was a wet paintbrush. A survey had showed that a majority of Limestone's schoolchildren believed that all lions were black. This worried the city council so much that they employed a man to paint the lion a golden colour to match the ones seen on television. There was an immediate uproar among those citizens who valued the occasional triumph of imagination over nature. A civic committee was appointed to return the sculpture to its original hue. A year later the tug-of-war continued. When the sun set the lion was a defiant yellow. By the time the sun rose it was black as the inside of a closet. Sometimes the two committees became confused. The sculpture, which for years had escaped the indignity of having gum stuck to its nose, ended up looking like a cheap blonde whose roots were showing.

Frank signalled to Savage and Fastboy not to wake the sleeping man. With one hand gripping the handles of his bicycle, Frank reached out with the other and patted the lion's nose. It was a hard life when everyone was trying to paint you a different colour. In one of the bicycle mirrors, Frank spied a tree festooned with ballons. They were the remains of a birthday party held in Independence Park that day in honour of a woman who was one hundred years old.

She'd spent the afternoon watching the balloons flap in the lake breeze. Some exploded as their skins were lanced by sharp branches while others would hang around for days shrivelling away to nothing. Better to go with a bang, thought the old woman as she tried to wheel herself into the path of an oncoming ice-cream truck.

It was Frank's idea to go fishing. The moonlight was a bright hook dipping into the lake.

– This is good, he smiled. Fish are attracted to the light.

– That's moths, corrected Savage.

– Fish too, insisted Frank.

– Too bad Cowboy isn't here, grunted Fastboy. He's the fuckin' expert.

– He don't eat fish, explained Frank. That would be cannabalism.

– You don't got to eat them to know how to catch them, countered Fastboy. Besides Cowboy don't got real fish in him. He just thinks he does.

– Where's the difference? said Savage.

When the lake iced over in winter some of the fish remained close to the surface. If the sun was out skaters were forced to navigate carefully to avoid tripping over a thin man wearing a woman's overcoat, his forehead pressed against the ice. People asked him what he was doing.

– I'm reuniting families, replied Cowboy.

They slid down the embankment underneath the bridge. Every action requires a jumping-off point and the bridge was a popular choice. It connected Limestone with provinces to the west. Two bridge-spans allowed tall ships to pass from the inner to the outer harbour. People fell into the habit of regarding it as a place of transition. The structure it replaced at the turn of the century was known as the Farthing Bridge. Although loved by the public, the city council felt it lacked the prestige a prosperous harbour city like

94

Limestone deserved. Plans were drawn for a new bridge. The structural engineer recognized that beyond the practical requirements there was a general need to convince the community that Limestone was entering the twentieth century in good faith. Unfortunately what most people objected to in the Farthing Bridge was what the engineer most admired. The strength of a man's desire to cross from point to point, whatever the obstacles, was encompassed in every beam and joint. The knot holes through which fishing poles could be inserted and then left while the fisherman snoozed, the boards that buckled under the weight of snow in winter provided the human touches that made the journey interesting. With more than a hint of sadness the structural engineer set about the task of creating an invisible bridge. One in which there were virtually no seams. It was to be the legacy of the engineer that unhappy men and women were drawn to that bridge. If you can't see where things join together it becomes harder to see where they've fallen apart.

The stench of rotting fish, seaweed and oil from the cars passing overhead was overwhelming.

– I don't know what we're doing here, grumbled Fastboy, stubbing his toe on a rock. We got no rod, no bait, the fish are dead.

The only equipment Frank needed was a safety pin, a length of string and a blind man's cane. In the north, where Frank spent his childhood, hunting and fishing were a man's alphabet. The basic skills you needed to survive. At dawn, when the mist was still thick, Frank and his father, Oswald, took their gear down to the lake. Lulled into drowsiness by the constant slap and tickle of water lapping against the rocks and the sweet smell of pine, Frank often fell asleep against his father's shoulder while waiting for the fish to bite. Oswald's flannel shirt was rubbed almost bare in patches from the pressure of Frank's cheek. He might be awakened by the pleading tones of a loon or the jerk of his

95

father's arm as a fish was reeled in. Punching it in the eye to stun it, Oswald quickly slit its throat. He had no patience for those who killed for pleasure or who prolonged suffering. He made an incision with his knife and extracted a wet jumble of guts. Secretly Frank was appalled to see the components of a living creature dismantled with the same precision with which he'd seen his father take apart a clock or a radio.

Sometimes on these expeditions they were joined by neighbourhood boys home on leave from the war overseas. Instead of taking the fish back to the house they cooked it in a heavy black skillet over an open fire. It was Frank's special task to remove Oswald's glasses when they became steamed from the heat and to polish them. They were sturdy, old-fashioned spectacles and it was Oswald's contention that they were made to measure. While waiting for the fish to cook, one of the boys might roll up his trouser leg and show Frank the puckered hole through which a bullet had entered and left. Another would sit crouched low, hands over his ears, as if, like Frank, he heard dim and distant voices. The young soldiers held their heavy overcoats a little above the fire in the hope that some of the cloving, smoky smell would tangle up amid the weave of the fabric. A souvenir of home to take back to the trenches.

The only fish Fastboy wanted to catch was the carp tattooed on Rosa's ass. It was so lifelike he expected to see it flopping around in the toilet whenever she took a piss. He watched as Frank removed his shoes and Savage looped a piece of string around a safety pin. Hustlers were easy to handle as long as you kept one hand on your money. When you know something's crooked you compensate and things end up even. But lunatics play by different rules. They erase half the world and draw in something completely different. A woman with the beak of a chicken or a train zooming out of a fireplace. A child sucking its thumb in the middle of a man's belly. According to Fastboy there was nothing about Frank's pregnancy that couldn't be cured with a few well-placed volts. And then there was Savage. A kid who killed things with one hand and supported the Virgin Mary with the other. You had to be crazy to walk a tightrope like that. Faith was something Fastboy's father packed away with the boxer shorts and the shaving cream and took with him when he left. Whenever Fastboy passed a church he saluted the ultimate hustler.

– God plays a shell game, he told Hatch. You point to the place you're sure he's hiding and there's nothing there. He's pulled a switch. It's the oldest profession in the world.

Fastboy could still see his mother on her knees night and day after his father left praying to God.

– He sees us in our distress, she told him.

When it came to choosing a hustle Fastboy chose blindness.

– Me and God, he said, all we see is the shape of a billiard ball floating across the table. We see the colour of money.

It wasn't intentional but when Fastboy spoke the words came out needles to prick Frank's confidence.

– Hey, Frank, he said, you don't need a fishing rod.

– How come? asked Frank.

– You're a holy man, answered Fastboy. You can just *walk* on the fuckin' water and cast your nets.

– Leave it out, warned Savage.

– You think God loves you, Frank?

– Oh yes, whispered Frank. I'm having a baby. I think that'a good sign.

– He don't love you, said Fastboy. He don't love a fat man shut like a cookie in the Loony Tin.

– You got more eyes than a potato, hissed Savage, and all they see is dirt.

– I got nothing against Frank, protested Fastboy, but

97

crazy is crazy. What's he going to do at the end of nine months and no baby?

In a voice that lived up to its name Savage answered:

– *I'll* be the fuckin' baby if I have to. I'll cry and wet my pants and suck on his tit.

– Yeah? said Fastboy. No hard feelings. We all need to curl up in a warm place sometime. Mine's over on the island. I just got to figure out how to get there.

– Since you're the wise man tonight, suggested Savage, why don't *you* just walk across the water?

– Walking on water is easy, declared Fastboy. The hard part is convincing other people it's not a trick.

While the other two were arguing Frank waded quietly into the water. The lake was cooler than the air and ink black. Frank thought he might emerge permanently discoloured. The stones on the bottom were sharp and jabbed the soles of his feet. When the water reached his waist Frank folded his arms over his stomach. He worried that one of Fastboy's remarks had punctured a hole where the water could rush in and drown the baby.

– The kick inside is matched by the kick outside, thought Frank.

A large green apple bobbed on the surface of the water where the reflection of Frank's face should have been. He picked it up and bit into it without noticing its soggy texture and sour taste. Frank wondered what the child thought about its imminent arrival. He pictured it swimming through a jungle of veins, up towards the hollow in his chest where the skin was thin and close to the bone. He saw the child cradled between his lungs, peeking out through the membrane. He felt the child's horror when it realized how close to the wreckage it was. The water tugged at his clothes like an eager child and Frank thought of it as his future son or daughter. The child had no desire to climb on to dry land and scavenge for food and shelter. It did not want to share Frank's uncertain life. Here in the water were apples and fish. Below the surface was a quiet place where harsh words couldn't follow. The waves would rock the baby to sleep at night. This was a good place to raise a child. The weight of the world reduced to nothing.

— Savage! he called.

— Yeah, Frank?

— I'm staying in the water, Savage, he said. Underneath, where there's peace.

— There's no breathing under the water, Frank.

— Things don't seem so heavy here.

— I know, agreed Savage. That's the good part of being dead.

Earlier in the day while hunting through scrap-heaps Savage came upon a disused jack-in-the-box. The lid was shut, the sides battered and the paint chipped. The box was decorated with scenes of circus life. Thinking that Frank might like to have it for the baby, Savage showed it to him.

— Look, said Frank, pointing to one of the pictures, a bear.

— And here's an acrobat, added Savage.

A portrait of Gonzino Bay in younger days.

— He looks like Victor Mature, remarked Frank.

— Who?

— Does it work? enquired Frank.

— I don't know, admitted Savage.

On the side of the jack-in-the-box was a crank. As it turned the toy emitted a harsh tinkle like the sound of marbles dropping onto glass. Finally the spring which held the lid was released. Instead of popping out, however, Jack remained resolutely in the box. Prying it open with a pen-knife Savage discovered a rusted coil decorated with the shredded remains of an acrobat's costume.

— It don't come out right, sighed Frank.

– I'll fix it, Frank. Don't worry.

As far as Savage could tell there was little difference between birds and men. Throw them a crumb and wait for them to pick it up.

– Listen, Frank, he said, let's show the kid birds. Fish are good, they move fast and light. But they're not as good as birds. We can go to the park, lie on our backs and look up at the sky. The kid won't feel so heavy then.

– You think so? asked Frank.

– Yeah, he answered. Besides, the sky don't freeze over in winter.

Without once checking his footing Savage found his way to Frank's despair. He promised pigeons for breakfast and toys for the baby.

Tangier as a Sketching Ground

It was no good trying to wriggle out of what you owed a dead person. A bony hand descended on your shoulder. A reproachful cough sounded in your ear. Their wills were iron clad. After church families trouped out to Limestone Cemetery to pay their respects. An elderly woman tried to picture the face of her dead lover and could think only of his feet. They were long and graceful. You could see the muscles when he moved. To be able to live with a man you had to be able to live with his feet.

– I could tell by his toes, she sighed, that we would be happy.

Then she spat on a lace handkerchief and attempted to rub away the graffiti daubed on the headstone by a vandal who thought death was violent and obscene anyway. Uncomfortable with tears, the men spoke to each other across the gravesites about business and the weather. Children kicked discarded cans in a makeshift game of soccer before being called to heel by their mothers. They spoke in hushed tones as though the dead were small animals easily frightened by raucous laughter or a good cry.

In the middle of the story about the headless man the bus driver deposited Maxine and Cowboy at the gates of the Limestone Cemetery.

– I wanted to know how it ends, complained Cowboy.

For a fleeting moment the bus' headlights illuminated the

caretaker's stone cottage before leaving it behind in darkness. Maxine shivered.

– It ends here, she said.

Cowboy found it peaceful to stand on the threshold of a place where everyone was dearly beloved.

From where they stood Maxine and Cowboy had a clear view of Limestone. The searchlights of the prisons swept the streets clean. From the centre of the city rose the spires of the university, an acrobat's nightmare. Going against the instructions of the church one of the masons had carved delicate flowers and mythical animals into the stone. It was a reminder to future generations of students that not everything carved in stone was a commandment. And overlooking the waterfront was City Hall. The first mayor of Limestone had a passion for fishing so when the City Hall was built he had it raised within spitting distance of the water. The limestone shimmered in the moonlight, providing extra light for the under-secretaries despatched to dig for worms in the garden. Nearly five hundred windows were installed as a favour to the mayor's brother-in-law, a window cleaner. The *Limestone Gazette* devoted an entire edition to discussing the merits of the dome roof. Visiting dignitaries bestowed nothing but praise although they were startled to see encased in purple stockings the fat legs of the mayor protruding from an upper window and a fishing line cast into the waters below.

– Hey, said Maxine, we should hold our breath.

– Why? asked Cowboy.

– It's so you don't hurt the feelings of the dead people, she explained, so they don't feel bad about not being able to breathe.

Cowboy considered this idea.

– If I was dead, he said, I wouldn't be jealous.

– For Chrissakes, she hissed, it's just a fuckin' superstition.

– You can't believe in stuff like that, said Cowboy.

– I never believed in luck 'til I lost it, replied Maxine, Now I don't take any chances.

The path through the cemetery was littered with wilted floral arrangements. Lily had refused to have flowers on her grave.

– Why watch something living fade and die all over again? she said. Why cover me with a replay of my own misfortune?

Cowboy suggested to Doris that they plant an apple tree over Lily. They were the only fruit she tolerated.

– Apples are bible fruit, she sighed, and you can't turn your back on that, I guess.

As the roots took hold it would give her something to consider, a connection with living things. The shoots would tap on the coffin like a telegraph from the outside world. In the years to come the roots would become stronger, piercing the wood and ripping away the satin lining like a frustrated lover. No more than bones, Lily could cling to those sharp fingers and pull herself up by the roots. Ancestral roots. In springtime blossoms would appear, the scent of them promising new life; then apples as red, curved and tempting as Lily in her favourite dress. Where there was a graveyard would now be an orchard. Sundays could be spent pruning, harvesting and climbing: ghosts of the departed swinging from the branches and building tree houses with their children and grandchildren. Instead, drunks slept among the headstones and woke up cold and stiff in the morning. The caretaker swept out the bodies of stray cats decomposing under the leaves. The only thing to be in a place like that was dead.

– My mother always said Old River would send me to an early grave, sighed Maxine.

– Hey, Maxine! cried Cowboy. I'll bet Lily's here.

— Lots of lilies here, she answered. Everyone here's a lily of the field.

— I'm going to look, declared Cowboy.

Maxine clutched at him.

— Let's go home, she pleaded. I got to find Old River.

— I been waiting twenty years, said Cowboy. I'm going to look.

— I don't want to be left alone.

— I'll come back, he said.

— Promise, she demanded. You got to promise.

— Wait for me at the gate, directed Cowboy.

— Concentrate on your breathing, urged Maxine. I don't give a fuck what the dead say. Think about your breathing, Cowboy.

There were hundreds of graves but only one would smell of almonds, peaches and jojoba. In a habit picked up from his mother Cowboy sniffed vigorously at each one. On the days when Lily's absence was especially felt Cowboy walked past the greengrocers and breathed deeply. Maxine leaned against the gate and watched him go. Here was a man who lived all his life next to an open grave and still travelled fearlessly among them to find the thing he'd lost. It moved her to see that wraithlike figure, a skeleton among skeletons, his bones exposed to harsher elements than wind and rain.

— Love's a broken bottle sometimes, she thought. It'll cut you down to nothing.

When Lily started to die in earnest her skin developed the porous texture of lemons. Looking into a hand mirror all she said was:

— I can't seem to get away from fruit.

She plucked at the clean white sheets (thinking they were geese) until they were threadbare.

– Cook 'em, begged Lily, it makes a change from Jello.

The head nurse was familiar with this sort of behaviour and replaced the sheets with a brown blanket. Lily stroked it (thinking it was a dog) and tried to teach it tricks. On the ceiling were pasted the orange footprints from the Arthur Frobisher Correspondence School of Dance. Lying side by side on their backs on the hospital bed Lily and Cowboy raised their legs and pretended to follow the steps of the dance.

– When I was little, she told him, I got taken to the circus. The only part that stays clear is the acrobats. A family with an Italian name. They were so high up I couldn't see the tight-rope. It was thin as this midnight wire that cuts into my brain and makes me remember. When they stepped from the platform I expected to see blood and bones below. But the acrobat just skipped across to the other side. It was the most beautiful thing I ever seen until you come along. My mother was always telling me to keep my feet on the ground. Being an acrobat looked like a better deal.

Nurses arrived with a trolley loaded with medication. They rolled up Lily's sleeve and drew blood in alarming amounts. Cowboy thought he could see in Lily's pale face the level of blood dropping as it was extracted. When the nurses left she grew listless and withdrawn. In an effort to keep Lily within easy reach Cowboy buried his head in her lap. She stroked his thin black hair.

– Play the game, he commanded.
– Baby, she sighed, you are simple as a guitar.
– Play the game!
– OK, she said. How many stars in the sky?
– I know! he shouted.
– How many voices in the world?
– I know!
– How many songs on earth and in heaven?

– I know! I know! I know!

Lily held Cowboy tight.

– Tell me then, she whispered, they might ask at the pearly gates.

In the evenings Doris stopped by the hospital to visit. She had never before seen so many beds in one place. Gradually her cheerful gossip slowed to a trickle and then stopped. Illness was a crystal ball into which Doris peered to gauge how bleak her future would be without Lily. Cowboy could tell Lily was dying from the look in Doris' eyes and hid under the bed until she'd gone. There he repeated his mother's name over and over to himself. He twisted the letters into a cord which would bind them together. Lily had showed him the cave where her breast used to be, the scar an ancient hieroglyph. It was a place where he had suckled and slept, a place of rest never denied to him in all his ten years. They both wept over their loss. At night Cowboy dreamed of pulling apart the injured skin and was surprised to find how close to the surface the heart now beat. It was a bird, impatient to be born, pecking its way to the surface.

– It will gobble up all the worms when I'm dead, said Lily, it will keep me whole.

Cowboy slipped through the incision he made in her skin. The blood was warm and juice red. Caught in an ebb and flow no intruder could divert, Cowboy was pulled towards Lily's heart. It acted as a giant mortar, pounding him into fine powder. There was no pain. It seemed a fitting end to be crushed by the weight of his mother's heart. When Cowboy was at last reduced to a mere speck he was free to float undetected through Lily's body. Now, wherever she went he would not be left behind.

★

The Preacher who presided over the burial service had driven from a neighbouring town in a beat-up Chevrolet. Doris had once attended a private service in the back seat of the Preacher's car and asked him to perform the ceremony. As they shook hands Cowboy noticed that the Preacher constantly wiggled his fingers. His face had the exaggerated length of a horse investigating a camera lens. The Preacher had brought his young son with him, a boy with golden curls and a tiny violin. He noticed Cowboy staring at the grape-sized wart on the underside of the Preacher's jaw.

– It's the mark of the devil, declared Ernie, and winked.

Overhearing this remark, the Preacher directed him to recite ten Hail Marys as penance.

– That's the wrong religion, whispered Ernie.

The Preacher was suffering from a severe cold and sniffled all the way through the short service. All Cowboy could concentrate on was the drop of liquid jiggling at the end of the Preacher's nose. He wondered whether it was going to splash down on the bible or be absorbed by the handkerchief the man kept in his breast pocket.

– It was sown a physical body, he sneezed.

– God bless, said Doris.

– Thank you, replied the Preacher, and it was raised a spiritual body.

In vain Cowboy waited for some manifestation of this spirit. A sign that a mother would come up through earth, tear down any wall to come back to her son. Ernie played "How Long Blues" on the violin but told the Preacher it was the 53rd Psalm.

– Come on, Cowboy, sobbed Doris when it was over.

– I'm waiting for Lily, he said. The Preacher said she was coming back.

– That's not for real, explained Doris, that's bible talk.

For over an hour Cowboy stood alone at the grave. He

was afraid to turn his back in case one careless movement erased all his memories of Lily. Finally the gravediggers, who had living families to return to, lowered the coffin into the ground. The dirt of Lily's twenty-eight years was unceremoniously thrown over her but Cowboy was unable to move. He felt pinned to the spot like a knife-thrower's assistant waiting for the act to begin. Every shovel of earth released another blade. When it was over and the last bit of earth was patted into place, Cowboy stepped forward. Where he had been standing was an outline made of knives. It said: I was here. Remember me.

★   ★   ★

Under the stars, Maxine bided her time until a cowboy came to escort her back home. A man who ten years ago sang songs of love in a yellow dress. Drops of sweat fell like kisses on her breasts.

– I'm giving away memories tonight, she whispered. Here's one for the dead.

Lying next to the river she and Adam Whitelake indulged in sticky moments of intimacy. They listened to the muffled grunts of animals scrabbling up the river bank.

– Oh baby, groaned Adam, *baby*!

– A year of knowing me, thought Maxine, and you can't do better than that?

Lazily trailing her hand in the river, Maxine felt the current pulling on her fingers. The water seemed hardly to move on the surface, while below there was a headlong rush for open spaces. Adam sensed that Maxine's attention was wandering and proudly flourished his ace card.

– I'll tell you autumn, he said.

– OK, she said.

He placed soft leaves between her thighs.

– Love colours, he whispered.

When the heart jumps inside a woman it almost always lands in the opposite direction to the one she planned.

Leaves and grass made an arabesque across Maxine's naked back. Using his tongue Adam carefully removed every trace of earth. It made him jealous to see on Maxine any impression other than the one he was making.

– Maxine, he said, was I first?

– Broken record, she complained.

– Was I the first? he repeated.

– Adam's always first, she sighed. Don't you read the bible?

– Will I be last?

– The river's last, she answered. It will rise and drown us. Drowned by love.

– That's your mother talking, he commented.

– My cards are on the table, she said. Read 'em and weep. Night was coming but neither of them had the strength to make the first move. Their resolve failed with the light. The moon hung in the evening sky as pale and quivery as a trumpet solo. They lapsed into a generous silence, which invited inside the sound of the wind dodging the rushes and the dry cough of a tractor in a faraway field. Maxine wanted to stretch out the moment and wear it like a necklace. A bright and showy trophy to throw in the faces of the people who said Adam Whitelake would bring her nothing but grief. With Adam's body thrown warm across her, Maxine knew without question that life would never be this perfect again.

– Kiss goodbye the curve of my knees, she whispered.

Adam plucked a reed from the bank and twisted it round and round Maxine's ring finger.

– Maxine, he said, will you marry me?

– What?

– You heard me.

– No, she replied.

– How come? he demanded.
– Because, she answered, I know you better than I know myself.
– To know me is to love me, said Adam.
– I don't want the responsibility, she said.
– I'm the man, he told her, I take care of *you*.
(HAH! is what she thought.)
– Kiss goodbye the curve of my arms, she murmured.
The river could carry the weight of a man fifty miles downstream but what good was strength when you didn't have the will to save yourself? Maxine drew her legs together and thought about a distant time when she'd called her body her own. She knew that if she and Adam got married they'd have to move to Limestone so that Adam could find work. She'd never been there but knew from geography lessons that it stood on the edge of a lake fed by this river. A former garrison town, old soldiers had approved the choice of limestone as building material. Enemy ships crossing the water saw only a smudge of grey on the horizon and, after flogging the navigator, turned around and went home. How could you find your way in a city like that? Maxine dipped her fingers in the water and then flicked them in the direction of Adam's forehead.
– What are you doing? he asked.
– I'm baptizing you, she said quietly. I'm giving you a new name.
– Why?
– So I'll always remember how I feel about you.
– Maxine?
– I'm calling you Old River, she said.
– Will you marry me?
– Yes.

★   ★   ★

The moon is mischievous in a graveyard. It throws light the way a ventriloquist throws his voice. It tries to convince people that inanimate objects have a life of their own. What in the reasonable light of morning are wheelbarrows, hedges and drainpipes become transformed at night into the ghosts of murdered children, jilted lovers and vengeful misers. Anxious not to disturb anyone, Cowboy crept silently among the headstones. The newer graves were marked with a functional white cross, compact and weather-resistant. They were inscribed with the name of the deceased and the year they died. On the older headstones were inscribed little poems and remembrances. They provided a pencil sketch of the dead. You knew that one grave held a "thrifty wife", in another a "faithful husband". Everyone was so virtuous that Cowboy wondered how in their day there could have been wars, poverty and corruption.

A cloud obscured the moonlight so that Cowboy was unable to read the inscriptions. Already he'd found he couldn't rely on a sense of smell to direct him towards Lily's grave. By this time the smell of almonds, peaches and jojoba would have disappeared. A scent is not as constant as a son and it was useless to expect it. He moved with difficulty from one grave to another. Here the grass was overgrown and laced with nettles. The families of these dead were themselves deceased and there was no one to tend the graves. The dates on the headstones read too far back into Limestone's history to include Lily. Cowboy straightened up and was about to turn back when he noticed two white, vaguely human shapes heaving among the shadows. An ordinary man unacquainted with ghosts might have followed the example of his heart and run fast. But Cowboy's sympathies were as transparent as the ghosts themselves. They found him a good listener and treated him well. It was only when one of the shadows rose, struck a match, lit a cigarette

III

and said, Pass me a fuckin' beer, that Cowboy knew they were dangerous. Even then he might have slipped away if the cloud had not rolled back and turned the moon on him like a spotlight. One of the shadows shrieked and dove behind a headstone. The other one came towards Cowboy scratching his belly. He wore a pair of boxer shorts and one of those caps that tractor companies give away as advertisements. He stuck his hand down the front of his shorts and kept them there as if he was helpless without something to keep hold of. His name was Duane. He was sixteen years old and already had the stolid look of a man who would always be known as Duane and didn't mind.

– What are you doin' here? demanded Duane, You fuckin' spying on us or what?

– I'm trying to find Lily, stammered Cowboy.

– You're meeting a *woman*? hooted Duane. I don't fuckin' *believe* it!

– My mother, explained Cowboy. She's dead.

– I can believe *that*, asserted Duane. One look at you is enough to kill anybody.

Then he threw his arms over his face and staggered about in imitation of someone who's seen something too horrible for words. From behind the headstone came the voice of Duane's girlfriend. Although she felt a flicker of compassion for Cowboy she knew enough to disguise it as boredom. In her books Duane was better than nothing.

– Let's go, she whined.

– In a fuckin' *minute*, he snarled, flicking his cigarette butt at Cowboy's feet.

In the dark one man's disability looks pretty much the same as any other. On a street in broad daylight nobody could mistake Duane for the Midnight Cowboy. This was honest fact. But in a graveyard in the middle of night there was nothing but attitude to distinguish one from the other. One shadow was a little thinner and limped when it walked, that's all. It drove Duane crazy to think that in front of his girlfriend Cowboy's weakness might be mistaken for his own. He could harvest an entire field of corn with the sun balanced on his head and not feel the ache. He could drink beer in quantities that would drown a cow. He could please a woman. Or anyway, he could please himself with a woman. On the day he turned thirteen he stood a man. His father handed him a shotgun and told him to shoot the family dog, who was old and lame. That dog had grown up year by year alongside Duane but childhood was finished. When he took aim Duane deliberately missed the heart by an inch so that all the boyhood things he loved, including the dog, died slow and painfully and he wouldn't want to remember them anymore. Looking at Cowboy backed against a headstone brought to mind that dog. Both of them had that look of mute appeal. A scrawny hope that Duane's better nature might prevail.

His first punch was little more than a tap but it was quick and that lent it the weight of a heftier blow. Cowboy fell back against the headstone. The shock of it knocked the wind out of him but Maxine's instructions came rushing back to him and he thought hard about his breathing. Each gulp of air was borrowed and then returned. Night played on Duane's side and hid the direction of the attacks. Soon Cowboy was face down on the ground with a foot pressing harder and harder into his shoulder. He pictured himself being flattened into a fillet of bones until he was peeled from the earth in some future excavation. Like a shopper in the supermarket Duane sought the tenderest joints. He poked and prodded and slapped so that the fish thrashed around inside Cowboy's head and made it ache. There was blood on his tongue. Duane squatted down and grabbed a fistful of Cowboy's hair. The ground tilted and swung into sky.

– I *hate* fuckin' freaks, hissed Duane.

– Please, whispered Cowboy.

– You do *not* please me, said Duane. You fuckin' *disgust* me.

Cowboy received a vicious slap across the face. He felt the prickled hair on Duane's sunburnt arm. His mind went back to a similar incident in childhood. He'd arrived home bloody and reeling after being set upon by neighbourhood children. Lily cleaned his cuts and held him until he stopped shaking.

– There's two ways of being scared, she said. The first is hurting yourself and the second is hurting other people. If someone beats up on you, remember that person is worse sick than you, Cowboy. Medicine will never find a cure for being scared of what life brings.

Then she kissed him and sang to him. The garden rooted in her skin enclosed him in a softly scented place. The light was switched off.

– Lily, sobbed Cowboy, Lily.

*   *   *

A dream sat cross-legged on Maxine's eyes and told a story. In a room there were two small pools like those found in a Turkish bath. Both were edged with ceramic tiles of china blue. In each pool a mannequin floated face upwards in the water. They were waxen, finely moulded and wore thin-lipped smiles. They bumped gently against the sides of the pool. Careful not to get wet, Maxine reached over and dragged a knife across the throat of the nearest mannequin. Dipping a toe into the water she drew it out red. At first she thought it was Old River's mouth gaping open and then she realized it was the gash she'd made in his neck. A snake slithered out of the hole, raised its body at the command of some invisible puppeteer, hissed at her and then vanished down the drain. The soul of Old River departing the body. Maxine shook with anger. Right from the start Old River had brought her to a place she didn't want to be. Dreams were no different. Leaving bloody footprints on the tiles Maxine padded over to the other pool. Here was a white body like the other but there was no need for knives. Maxine knew that even if the wound was invisible she was responsible for a serious injury just the same. This was true since the body belonged to Cowboy. Real roses bloomed in his cheeks and he had a lovesick expression in his eyes. Somehow this upset Maxine more than the murder of her own husband. A watery grave was all Cowboy expected from this life but it was less than he deserved. Convinced that he was only holding his breath to punish her Maxine dove into the pool. She grabbed him by the shouders and shook him hard.

– Breathe, Cowboy! she screamed. I'm not the one who's dead so just you fuckin' BREATHE!

Nine Moons Wasted

After City Hall was built the council luxuriated in its vast dimensions. Their previous headquarters had been in the rear parlour of Limestone's chief architect. The central room of City Hall was so enormous that aldermen amused themselves by flying kites during council meetings. However, the treasurer pointed to the high cost of maintaining the building solely for their own prestige. Since it was an election year new taxes could not be introduced. An alternative was proposed. For six days of the week the unused portions of the building would be taken over by local farmers and used as a covered market. On the seventh day the rooms would be given to Limestone's various religious groups. Despite the stray cows wandering into board meetings, and the arguments between the Presbyterians and the Methodists as to who had the better choir, the arrangement was enshrined in Limestone's charter.

Clinging to the weather vane atop City Hall, Gonzino Bay imagined himself made of diamonds. Not chips of hard-edged shining but rocks still black and sweating from the earth. Every move he made scratched away at the world until the only thing left was Gonzino Bay: hard, solid, brilliant.

– I'll reduce this place to ashes, he said quietly, I'll be the goddamned Rock of Ages.

★

116

– Do you see something? asked Frank.

– Where?

– On top of City Hall.

– No, replied Savage, I can't see anything.

– I thought maybe it was an angel, said Frank. It could be a sign.

– No Parking's a sign, reminded Savage.

They'd left Fastboy behind, flexing his muscles and preparing to swim to the island. Frank had tried to persuade him not to go.

– You'll drown, he pointed out. It's too far for a blind man.

– If everyone could see the distance they had to travel in one lifetime, answered Fastboy, nobody would budge an inch.

– Well, considered Frank, are you sure?

– I'll be there before the baby comes, smirked Fastboy.

– Push off, said Savage. Happy landings.

Over the back entrance to City Hall was a hand-painted sign which read: Strictly Baptist Chapel Beulah. Underneath it were two teenage boys. They were black as spent matches. They were singing. Frank stopped to listen and felt the music fluttering soft as butterflies around him.

– What was that song? enquired Frank when they'd finished.

– "Sometimes I Feel like a Motherless Child", answered the youngest. Say amen!

– Amen, replied Frank. Who's Beulah?

– What's happening here? interrupted Savage.

– We're waiting for the service to start, said the older boy.

– Our father's giving the sermon, added his brother.

– Church at this time of the morning? queried Savage. It's close to four o'clock.

– No competition, said the oldest, we got a clear line to God.

– You are welcome to stay, he added.

– Let's go, Frank, urged Savage.

– I want to stay, said Frank.

– I thought you said you were hungry.

– The food I need doesn't have feathers, said Frank.

– OK, said Savage, but remember the church throws babies into water. I already saved you from that once tonight.

– You are the best voice I got, Savage, sighed Frank.

The chapel was in the east wing of City Hall. During the week farmers auctioned off their livestock here. The pews were high-backed wooden benches. By inserting a slat of plywood at regular intervals they were converted into pens for cattle and prize-winning pigs. Wisps of straw stuck to the knees of the congregation as they prayed. The pulpit was the auctioneer's stand. In moments of high emotion the Reverend was known to use the gavel for emphasis as if prepared to offer salvation to the highest bidder. Behind the pulpit were four stained-glass windows representing each of the basic food groups. The Reverend wore a simple black tunic but two of his teeth were gold. He did not fill the room but drew the room and all inside it, including Frank and Savage, into himself. One moment Frank felt he was bone, blood and sinew and the next nothing more than a drop of sweat on the Reverend's forehead.

– Welcome to our church, he said. There is a balm in Gilead.

Frank opened his mouth to reply but changed his mind. His own way of speaking sounded hard and contained in comparison with the Reverend's. You could bleed to death if caught on the corners of it.

The congregation numbered about two hundred. Next to Frank was an old woman and her grandson. If Frank shut

his eyes he could see, between the lid and the eyeball, the
exact colour of their skin: black with a hint of yellow. Gravity would soon call the old woman home. She squeezed
Frank's hand.

– Sweet, sweet Jesus, she murmured.

People left off private conversations and took their seats.
The atmosphere of suppressed excitement revealed itself in
the jubilant colours of the women's outfits: cerise, canary
yellow, pea green. Faith was a joyous thing to them and a
necessary thing.

– Brothers and sisters, intoned the Reverend.

It began quietly. The Reverend opened the Bible resting
on the lectern in front of him. A piece of straw was caught
between the pages and the Reverend picked it up and
chewed on it in a ruminative manner. Then he stepped back
from the lectern and strolled around in front of it. Their
impression was that he was an ordinary man who did not
separate himself from the trials of his congregation. He
knew their struggles and sympathized. For the moment he
was only a storyteller choosing a tale to fit the occasion.
The Reverend spoke of Lazarus brought back from the dead
for the benefit of those who did not believe.

– And Mary went to Jesus, he told them, saying, If you
had been here our brother Lazarus would still be alive. So
Jesus said to her: Take me to where he is buried. Which she
does, her heart leaping in hope. They stand at Lazarus' grave
and fall silent. Being human they would all like to see a
miracle but nobody believes for one second it will happen.
Dead is dead. And Jesus said, I will call three times. The
first time was real quiet. Lazarus. The second time was a
bit pleading. L-a-a-azarus!

The Reverend took the tone of a mother entreating an
errant child to come out of hiding. The less orthodox of
the congregation laughed out loud at his playfulness. Even
the older ones were amused by what the religious editor

of the *Limestone Gazette* had called, "a scandalous approach to the reading of scriptures".

– But the third time, continued the Reverend, Jesus spoke with all the force of heaven. LAZARUS! And Lazarus rose up and was restored to life. I will tell you that the non-believers switched sides with a speed wondrous to behold. And Mary fell at Jesus' feet and He lay His hand on top of her head and told her, Mary don't you weep. Brothers and sisters, faith is *powerful* medicine.

The congregation listened attentively. They gnawed on the bones of each word spoken, looking for some meat to sustain them through the coming week. The grandmother swayed to and fro. The stiff cloth of her blouse scratched Frank's arm. Someone clapped their hands and shouted. All *right!* Behind Savage a woman was moaning. It was a sound he heard often coming from the bushes in the park where he lay catching pigeons. Righteousness worked on some women the way whiskey worked on others. It opened them wide.

The Reverend retreated behind the lectern. The congregation sensed a change in the temper of the sermon. Until now the Reverend had tossed words like balls into the air and caught them before they hit the ground. But these new balls were being pitched, not tossed. His words hit the ceiling and ricocheted off the floor. They whizzed like ecclesiastical ammunition past the ears of a shell-shocked congregation. Frank's neighbour raised her arms above her head but whether it was to catch the words or protect herself from them he couldn't tell. The Reverend spoke, Jesus died and Frank felt personally responsible. And then the room shouted Hallelujah!, Jesus rose again and Frank was glad. The choir wove their voices into a basket into which they put pride, sorrow, joy and offered it up to God. Their voices dug graves out of which to rise glorious and new. Their voices shot up like a fountain and the water rained down on them and made them clean. Old men slapped their knees and shouted *Yes, Lord*! Women clung to each other and wept. Children swung their hips and snapped their fingers to the fervent wail of a saxophone. The noise of their celebration raised the roof and revealed the heavens in all their glory. This was seismic faith. It shook the foundations of Frank's world. These people did not need to see God to know that He existed. They loved one another in the silver time of night and that was enough. They saw their babies playing contentedly at their feet and that was enough. When all the voices shouting in their ears threatened to tear them apart one voice raised itself above all others and healed them. They praised Him and held Him to their hearts just as Frank longed to do with his baby inside him. He wanted to cradle in his arms something clean and trusting. He wanted a child to save him. Frank reached out and touched the shoulder of the old woman who was down on her knees rocking and praying.

– I'm going to have a baby, he said.

Gently she pulled Frank down beside her and laid a work-worn hand on top of his. Their joined hands, like the keys of a piano, played a soothing melody. Maybe this church was another kind of hospital. Certainly people seemed to be in a world of their own. They whooped and hollered and danced to a private music. But the food was better and you got wine with your meals. Frank didn't know much about religion but craziness he could write a book about. He was no more of a lunatic than anyone else in the room. As all around him people celebrated a miracle, Frank felt Savage's thin arms encircle him, holding him upright.

Five Blind Boys from Alabama
Kick up their Heels

Amid the overgrown grass of the Limestone cemetery crickets rubbed their crooked legs together and made a kind of music. Cowboy wished that he could do the same. Painfully he rolled over on his back and blinked up at the stars. If this was dying he wanted his soul to go up, not down. For a second he thought he saw a transparent replica of himself flickering above him. The weedge-weedge of the crickets became the plinking of harp strings. Enormous wings filigreed with gold beat above his head. But then he noticed a pointed rock digging into his buttocks. He felt the bruised-apple flesh along his ribs.

– Say goodbye to heaven, ordered Mrs Munscher.

– What are you doing here? murmured Cowboy.

– You're lying on my grave.

IDA MUNSCHER
b. 1922 d. 1969
Loving wife and mother

It shook Cowboy's faith in the sanctity of remembrance.

– Sorry, he apologized.

– These things happen, she responded charitably.

– I haven't had much luck tonight, he sighed.

– I lived a whole life like that, snorted Mrs Munscher.

– Did you know this was going to happen? demanded Cowboy.

– Don't use that tone of voice with *me*, countered Mrs Munscher (loving wife and mother), I warned you.

Lying at the base of her headstone was an empty cigarette carton. Mrs Munscher swooped down, picked it up and handed it to Cowboy.

– I hate litter bugs, she said. Throw this in the garbage on your way out.

– Am I going? he asked weakly.

– Do I want you lying on my grave for the rest of your natural born days? I think not.

With the ruthlessness of a marine drill sergeant Mrs Munscher nudged Cowboy until he was on his feet.

– Goodbye, he said.

– Goodbye, said Mrs Munscher.

★　★　★

– What's up, Cowboy? mumbled Maxine sleepily.

– The moon, he answered, the stars.

– No game, she said. What happened?

– Not everyone here is dead, he told her.

Under one eye was the promise of a plum bruise.

– I almost saw heaven, he confided.

– You don't want to die in a graveyard, scolded Maxine. Nobody would notice.

– You would, said Cowboy.

– Only if I tripped over you.

– Maxine, you know that acrobat?

– No, she said.

– The one I saw tonight on the roof, persisted Cowboy.

– Oh yeah, she yawned. So?

– Maybe he's an angel, ventured Cowboy.

– You can't see angels, explained Maxine. They're invisible. You only hear them. One lives in your left ear and tells you to do good things and the other lives in your right ear and tells you to do bad things.

    – How do you know?

    – I just know, she said.

    – I thought angels lived in heaven, said Cowboy.

    – I think when you die they leave your head and go back up to God. Maybe they have to fill in a report about how many times you listened to the devil.

    – Like at the welfare? asked Cowboy.

    – Maybe.

    – I can't do tests, Maxine.

    – Don't worry, she said. You'll do OK.

    – What about you?

    – Me? she laughed. I haven't got a prayer.

    – I'll pray for you, Maxine.

    – Come on, Cowboy, she sighed. Let's go home.

    – What about Old River?

    – He's home now, she said.

    – You sure? asked Cowboy.

    – Yeah, said Maxine.

★   ★   ★

Old River was dead. In a room this small there was no escaping a fact like that. Most of the blood was dried in a red collar around his neck, but you could tell that it had gushed out at first by the way some of the blood had splattered across the rest of his body. It showed up defiant against the whiteness of his skin. Some of the blood had dried a dusky rose and was smeared on his arms and legs and across his distended belly. All the defects of Old River's body were accentuated and preserved. His toenails needed a trim.

When they reached No. 22 Colbourne Street Maxine paused at the doorway.

124

– What colour are your eyes, Cowboy? she asked.

– Brown, he answered. You know that.

– I can only see the whites, she told him. So is it me that's blind or you?

– Take it easy, Maxine.

They climbed the stairs to her room.

– I'm blind, she muttered, and I never used to be.

When they got upstairs Maxine unbuttoned her shirt and slipped out of her jeans. By the time Cowboy dragged his eyes away from the corpse she'd rolled her clothes into a bundle and thrown them on the floor of her closet. All she wore was a bra and a pair of black cotton underpants. The material of the bra had worn thin with use over the years and the outline of her nipples was clearly visible. To his shame Cowboy felt a thumpety-thump in a part of his anatomy also worn thin over the years.

– What are you doing? he asked.

– Someone's bound to call the police, she replied. I got to get the fuck out of here.

Nobody held anything against Maxine but they'd already known the stench of a body left too long in the house. Maxine removed a yellow dress from a hanger. It was wrinkled and the days of a perfect fit were gone.

– Everything I remember is stretched out of shape, she moaned.

The dress acted the way a bright light does on an actor who's known better days. It showed the wrinkles, the bad diet and the wrong decisions.

– I don't understand, Maxine, said Cowboy. Where was love when you did this?

– OK, agreed Maxine, this is my pushing-off note. I'll tell you.

She motioned to Cowboy to come closer, so that he stood within reach on the other side of the bed. Then Maxine stretched out her arms over the corpse until her fingertips

125

were just touching Cowboy's. Then she shut her eyes. This was the only way she would reveal her secrets. Touching the person reassured Maxine that there was someone listening, but not seeing them convinced her that she was giving nothing away.

    – It was all right at first, she began. When the snake was sleeping, Old River could be sweet. We invented colours and that was good. When we come here to the city I was missing home but Old River was happy. After he got the job at the supermarket stocking shelves he'd tear off the silver labels from soup cans and bring them to me. Or he'd find a blade of grass half burned into gold by the sun and put it on my tongue. That's what I expected from love and it didn't seem so much.

    Cowboy nuzzled her fingers as a signal to continue.

    – The problems started after he lost his job. You know how Old River was when he got into work. He loved being everywhere and doing everything. I seen him and I knew he made himself too familiar. That manager couldn't wait to fire him. After that the snake never slept quiet and I got too tired to watch it all the time. You seen him, Cowboy. Old River just got to sitting on the bed with whatever stuff he could afford out of the welfare cheque. Or he'd be down at the Plaza or with those fuckin' dogs. He got mean and dirty and expected me to recognize the man I married every time he come to bed.

    – About a year ago, she said, I started losing colours. I woke up and looked at the carpet and I knew it used to be orange but all I could see was white. At first it was things just here and there. A tree might turn white or somebody's mouth. Then it got to be more and more. This whole month I practically seen nothing but white. I tried to tell Old River but he just called me crazy. Spread open my legs and said how I had enough colour to keep *him* happy. The last couple of days I've been sitting here thinking and thinking about the way it was before. And it seemed to me that it was mostly Old River's fault the way things turned out. Every time I got ready to leave, that snake twisted me around and I ended up in the same old place. When Old River come in tonight I went over to make him do something about it, only he was passed out cold. But I was remembering about Arctic explorers, how they'd get lost in the snowstorms and start walking around in circles. And it come to me what I had to do. I got out Old River's hunting knife. It wasn't very sharp so it took a couple of tries but when the red finally come it was lovely. I sat beside him and watched the red start to mix with the white so soon there was pink. Three colours. I started to feel a lot better. I even started to like Old River a little because he give me those colours. The thing is that everything started to get mixed up in my head and I got to where I couldn't see Old River anymore. I got to thinking that he must have sneaked down to the Plaza when I wasn't looking. That's when I come down to you. I see things clear now, Cowboy, and I'll tell you something, nobody knows how to love me right. Not even me.

Light was sneaking into the room.

– The whole night spent looking for a dead thing, sighed Cowboy.

– Yeah, said Maxine.

Rummaging in a drawer, Maxine found a pair of scissors. She used them to cut out a small square of material from the hem of her dress.

– It's all I got to give you, she apologized.

– I'm coming with you, declared Cowboy.

– Think straight, she said. What am I supposed to do with a cripple?

– I'll be lonely for you, he cried.

– A killing ends more than one life, Cowboy.

– I love you, Maxine.
– Thank you, she said.

Shapes were emerging in the twilight in the way a pencil rubbed across paper reveals the outline of the object underneath. Colbourne Street was still shuttered and silent except for the snoring of Doris and Hatch. They were curled up asleep on the doorstep. Maxine almost tripped over them on her way out.

Hatch's tufted head rested against Doris' breast. Her legs were slung across his lap. They were wound around each other like dogs on a cold night looking for comfort. Doris was always forgetting her key to the house. She trusted in people to accommodate her eccentricities. Gingerly Maxine lifted a corner of Doris' wig and slid her own key underneath. As she replaced the hairpiece Doris opened one eye a crack.

– The sun's up, she croaked.
– It's only my dress, explained Maxine. Go back to sleep.
– You coming or going? asked Doris.
– You tell me, said Maxine.
– Do I snore? asked Doris. I always wanted to know.
– Listen, Doris, whispered Maxine. I done a dirty thing.
– What?
– I killed Old River.
– Oh, said Doris.
– Blue into side pocket, murmured Hatch.
– I know a woman done the same thing, said Doris. Blacked out one night and when she woke up her husband was dead on the kitchen floor with an icepick through his eye. People asked me did I think she was guilty? I said: Married's a tough life. Besides, I liked her tattoos.
– I stood here fifteen years ago, said Maxine. I was saying hello.

– Hello, Maxine, smiled Doris.

– Hello, Doris, said Maxine.

With every step Maxine took, the streets appeared to stretch and then shrink. It tricked the mind. Maxine wasn't sure whether she was really moving, or standing still and it was the street that was falling behind. She dragged her hand along limestone walls and fingered the dips in the stone. It must be torture for prisoners to live in buildings made of limestone. It looked so soft a sharp tongue could cut through it but when you pressed against it the stone refused to yield.

– It's me that's weak, thought Maxine.

She snuck by Libra's, afraid that someone would see her. But outside the Plaza she stopped and pressed her forehead against the door. The cuts that Old River had made with his knife scratched her skin. The management would replace the door and there would be nothing left to say that he'd been here. You could cut the air with your finger. You could cut the air with a knife. Either way it was hard to make your mark in this world.

When Maxine got to the bridge there was only one other person in view. The way his body was angled kept his face partly hidden. She noticed the jaw, once broken, that never mended properly so that it sort of swung on its hinges. She recognized the lean legs of the boy that stayed loyal to the man.

– Adam Whitelake, she said.

– I been waiting, Maxine.

– I still got meat on my bones, she said, in case you had thoughts about worrying me to death.

– Look at the lake, he said. You can hardly tell which is sky and which is water. This was always your best time of day.

– Adam, she said.

– Not Adam, he said. I never been first in nothing. Not in my whole life.

– First with me, replied Maxine.

– Look where it got me, responded Old River. Dead dead dead.

– I'm sorry, apologized Maxine, that's the truth.

– You *named* me, cried Old River. A river can't choose its own nature.

He pointed to the wounds already healed into scars. The skin was ridged and sensitive.

– It's easy to rip a human being apart, he said. Both of us forgot that.

The only breeze blowing was Maxine's hot breath.

– Come here, she said.

– What for? he asked.

– I want you to dance with me.

– What?

– No one's lookin', she said.

There was a shyness between them in the way of men and women who haven't acknowledged to each other their common desire.

– I was never good at dancing, Maxine.

– Dancing is two people knowing each other, she told him. I lived with you fifteen years. I licked the salt off your skin. I named you. And I killed you. Come here and dance with me.

Flesh and spirit wedded by a gold ring and a hunting knife. Old River moved inside her like the old days when they used to lick the maple syrup off the ground after loving each other. Maxine was always convinced that her vital organs would be displaced. Loving a man made you feel crowded and crumpled inside and then it left you empty. A car rolled over the bridge. It slowed down when it came to Maxine but didn't stop.

– Let's get out of here, whispered Old River.

– I asked that for fifteen years, said Maxine. I should have killed you sooner.

– I always loved that dress, whispered Old River.

– I thought you were gone for good, she said, and nothing but your name for company.

– I'm *waiting*, Maxine.

It wasn't Maxine's life that flashed before her eyes. It was a blind man's cane floating out towards the island.

– Oh, shit, she said.

Her yellow dress billowed out over the water. It was like the sinking sun.

Edna St Vincent Millay
Sitting under a Tree

Ernie awoke from a deep sleep to find the face of Gonzino Bay shining like the full moon through his window. Having been raised in a religious environment Ernie was well acquainted with the notion of miracles and holy signs. A divine visitation was not totally unexpected. On the other hand, being told constantly that you were a base sinner and unworthy of witnessing the Lord's more imaginative moments undermined a man's confidence. Under ordinary circumstances Ernie might have rolled over and gone back to sleep. Fortunately for Gonzino Bay a lengthy acquaintanceship with tequila also paves the way for all kinds of unexplained phenomena. Ernie padded over to the window and assisted Gonzino Bay inside.

– The city roofs aren't as easy to navigate as in my great-grandfather's day, confessed Gonzino Bay. Between television antennae, satellite dishes and attack parrots . . . frankly, I'm unnerved.

– I watched you practising earlier, said Ernie, on the roof of the Plaza Hotel.

– That was you?

– Yes, admitted Ernie. I dreamed of flying.

– Well, said Gonzino Bay modestly, that's my job.

– What is? asked Ernie.

– To provide a new perspective.

The room was barely large enough to accommodate the two men. The organ along with various other instruments took up most of the space. Ernie sat on the armchair, a broken spring made it unsuitable for guests, while Gonzino Bay settled on the bed. On the floor were stacks of books bound in drab colours and prefaced with lengthy explanations about the typesetting. They had serious titles like, *The Significance of the Nose in Renaissance Literature* or *A Comprehensive History of the Toothpick.* Ernie picked up one of the volumes.

– It touches me, he said, that people write these books. I think it must come as a shock to them to find that the world doesn't share their passion. It's a larger place than they imagine.

Outside, a gate clanged shut. A woman, speaking in a foreign tongue, shouted endearments, warnings and the names of her children at the retreating figure of her husband.

– This is my favourite part of the city, mused Gonzino Bay. I love to watch the Italian woman at home, the centre of her family. There she rules the roost without question. But when she steps out of the house, to the supermarket or the department store, she becomes nervous. Among people speaking only English she feels inadequate, hesitant, always smiling. In her own home she has the confidence to be bad-tempered sometimes. You can only properly be angry in a language that other people understand. Otherwise what's the point? Nothing is accomplished.

A pigeon landed on the windowsill. It poked its head in and out pecking lazily at the peeling paintwork. The two men studied the bird with the concentration which comes with extreme sleepiness. After a minute or two the bird flew away.

– If Savage was here, apologized Ernie, I could have offered you pigeon pie.

– Who is Savage?

– A boy who feeds us, answered Ernie.

133

– You know, began Gonzino Bay, there is a reason for my visit.

– Really? said Ernie. What is it?

– Our organist has left to become a lion tamer, sighed Gonzino Bay. It was on the cards. My wife Alice says that he has no music to soothe the savage breast and will be eaten within two days.

– I'm sorry, commiserated Ernie, but what has it got to do with me?

– I heard you playing the organ two nights ago, said Gonzino Bay.

He laid a tentative finger on the instrument. He knew how possessive musicians could be.

– I would like to offer you the job.

– Why me? asked Ernie. There are at least two other organists in the city who would jump at the chance.

– I think, replied Gonzino Bay, you understand what I need. I'm getting to be an old man and sometimes a night's work is more than I can bear. When I step out on that platform I don't want curlicues of music played by a man whose nose is buried in a tabloid newspaper. I want music played by someone who appreciates the significance of my memories. When I hear a Bach organ concerto or "Peg o' My Heart" I need to be lifted back to a time when I was strong and my eyesight good.

– I appreciate your faith in me, sighed Ernie, but I can't accept your offer.

– Why? begged Gonzino Bay. Is it the money?

– Oh no, replied Ernie. You see I never allow my music to go as high as God. I make a ceiling that the notes can't rise above. You might bump your head on it. The audience would see your limitations.

– I understand, said Gonzino Bay sadly, and after a moment added: then could you please direct me to the nearest bus stop?

– Of course, said Ernie, and led him to the window.

Together they looked out over a city that had long ago lost the habit of looking upwards.

Twists like a Crooked Pin

There's a slippery place where waking slides into sleeping. It was here that Midnight Cowboy lost his balance and flew across the room, arms and legs akimbo. The day's events were scattered to the winds. Spice-hot pain dripped from the ceiling onto the blue of his bed. Cowboy found himself surrounded by small red fish who swam to him open-mouthed. They told him stories.

– You sent me fish, Maxine, he complained.

– They come from Old River, she said. I can't help where they land.

– OK, he sighed.

Maxine was stretched out on top of the wardrobe. Strands of seaweed were caught in her hair. The lower part of her body was the tail of a fish.

– I thought you were gone, said Cowboy.

– What's lost gets found, she answered. You told me that.

The light above Cowboy's bed swung back and forth like a hypnotist's gold watch. Gonzino Bay shot out of the closet, performed two back somersaults and crashed into the wall. He rubbed his head.

– This is unfair, complained Gonzino Bay, that I should pay for your lack of imagination.

– I'm sorry, apologized Cowboy. What would you like?

– Well, considered Gonzino Bay, I would like, just once, to cross a tightrope without having to consider the possibility of falling.

– It must be a wonderful feeling, said Cowboy, to walk a thin line and not worry.

– I think so, agreed Gonzino Bay.

At the organ sat Ernie. He cracked his knuckles and tossed the tails of his tuxedo behind him.

– I will play "Ain't Misbehavin'", he announced, in a minor chord. I will be accompanied by Doris.

She wore a hat made of pastry. Her shoes were mismatched.

– I sang on my wedding night, she said. My husband threw a pan of water out the window. He thought it was cats.

The furniture was made of limestone.

– Hello, Cowboy, said Lily.

– Where have you been?

– Play the game, she said.

– How many glasses of whiskey make me drunk? he asked.

– I know! she cried.

– How many lies do lovers tell?

– I know!

– How many kisses heal a wounded man?

– I know! I know! I know!

Gonzino Bay was gliding across a high wire strung across the room.

– I always wanted to do that! exclaimed Lily.

– There's nothing to fear! cried Gonzino Bay. Climb up.

– I shall play "That Daring Young Man on the Flying Trapeze", announced Ernie.

Doris was eating her hat.

– Are you leaving? cried Cowboy.

– It's too hot here, explained Lily. I'm used to cooler climates.

– I'm alone, whispered Cowboy. I need you.

– Love doesn't need a shape, Cowboy, said Lily. What can be held can also slip through your fingers.

– Are you coming? asked Gonzino Bay.

– Yes! cried Lily.

The window blew open. The air smelled faintly of almonds, peaches and jojoba.

The Essential Trick

T he streetlights were being extinguished. Milk bottles clinked against doorsteps. Dogs crept exhausted under porches after running through the streets all night. Copies of the *Limestone Gazette* were meticulously folded to enable newsboys to throw them accurately into geranium beds. The smell of baking bread began to seep through the back streets. At a place where the aroma was strongest Savage stopped and knocked. A man opened the door and instructed Savage to wait. Inside the thud of soft dough being kneaded in giant mixers mingled with cries for more flour and compassion for the baker's unsteady hand. After a minute the man returned and handed Savage a large bag of breadcrumbs. The cook at Libra's offered these in exchange for a catch of pigeons. Later they would be miraculously transformed into chicken pie.

The morning air had the frail, sticky quality of a cobweb. Anything that moved was caught and held to be devoured by the greater heat of the day. Savage pointed to some pigeons sleeping on the grass. He instructed Frank to lie down. Reaching into the bag Savage scattered some bread-crumbs in the direction of the birds. The idea was to make a trail which they would follow. After dropping some more crumbs at his feet Savage lay down beside Frank and began to concentrate. All his energies were directed towards the pigeons. His ears measured the time it took for the birds' soft trills to reach him. His heart slowed down so that long waits were bearable. Through long practice Savage had gained the skill of breathing in shallow hiccoughs so that he appeared almost lifeless. It was this that had fooled Frank when they first met and even now Frank shook him vigorously sometimes just to make sure. The nerves in Savage's fingers were distinct from each other in the way that the coils of an electric stove are separate but burn together. Next to him Frank was wheezing and picking stray crumbs out of his beard. The pigeons noticed this movement and doubled back to their original position. Savage sat up slowly and threw them some more bread. He was suspicious of the silence that lay around the park. It was laced with hints of sudden noises.

In one of the houses on the rim of the park a baby began to cry. Out of the corner of his eye Frank noticed Savage purse his lips in exasperation. The baby seemed to be unsure of what kind of noise to make. Through the open window came deep-throated gurgles. Then there was a series of staccato bursts which ended with a full-blown yell. It was a cry of pure longing untempered by politeness. Men and women grew up and lost the habit of letting loose a howl like that. Most of the time their needs were no different from a baby's. A light in the house was switched on. Frank imagined the mother, frazzled from lack of sleep, scooping up the baby in her arms and jiggling it roughly, urging quiet. As the baby continued to cry she unbuttoned the neck of her nightgown and offered her breast, to which the baby had given a new form and function. The baby's yell reversed into silence as mother and child nourished each other. Frank snuggled up to Savage.

– You know, Savage, he whispered, before I knew you I used to watch you sometimes. I'd be riding on my bicycle and I'd look out for you. You were hard to spot sometimes you'd be lying so quiet but then maybe I'd catch a glimpse of those white sneakers of yours. I knew a bird was close when your shoulders started to hunch off the ground from the waiting. And when the bird finally got near I seen the way you grabbed at it and when you did, I knew that bird was dead.

– Frank, hushed Savage, you gotta be quiet or they won't come. You can't think about anything but getting those birds to come close to you. There's a fat one eyein' me right now. I want that bird but I gotta want it more than anything else or it won't come.

The pale moon loitered. It was unwilling to give up its position to the rising sun.

– Do you think the others are right? asked Frank anxiously. About the baby I mean. Do you think I'll have to go back to the hospital?

– Frank, that bird is about one breath away from me.

– Please tell me what you think about my baby.

Savage fingers buried in feathers.

– I think it's going to be a fucking beautiful kid, Frank.

When the pigeon met its fate Frank never knew it. He was feeling the baby move inside him. He was thinking of names.